He stroked her hair gently and bent to kiss her neck. Cassidy squeezed her eyes shut tight and begged herself to find a way to stop her world from spinning out of control. Eric's mouth was next to her ear, and she could hear his breath growing heavier with excitement. There was no way she could go through with this. Things had already gone too far.

THE SECRETS OF BOYS

Hailey
ABBOTT

AVON BOOKS

An Imprint of HarperCollins*Publishers*

The Secrets of Boys
Copyright © 2006 by Alloy Entertainment
All rights reserved. Printed in the United States of America. No
part of this book may be used or reproduced in any manner what-
soever without written permission except in the case of brief quo-
tations embodied in critical articles and reviews. For information
address HarperCollins Children's Books, a division of
HarperCollins Publishers, 1350 Avenue of the Americas, New York,
NY 10019.

www.harperteen.com

ALLOYENTERTAINMENT   Produced by Alloy Entertainment
151 West 26th Street, New York, NY 10001
Library of Congress Catalog Card number: 2005906569
ISBN-10: 0-06-082433-6 – ISBN-13: 978-0-06-082433-4
Typography by Joel Tippie
❖
First Avon edition, 2006

Chapter One

Cassidy Jones wished her best friend, Larissa King, were Amish at times like these. It would have made life a lot easier, especially when it came to going to parties. Instead of obsessing over which pair of jeans to wear (either the low-waisted, boot-cut Citizens of Humanity ones that make her appear to have a butt, or the stretch, dark True Religion ones that were perfectly broken in), Cassidy could spend her time burying her nose in her sketchbook and drawing while sitting on the beach in Malibu. But that was not her fate today. She was about an hour away from attending a Pepperdine University party with Larissa, and Cassidy knew all too well what that meant. Soon Larissa would be acting the *opposite* of Amish—smoking, drinking, dancing, and perhaps even sexing it up with some college hottie. As for Cassidy, she was preparing for another night spent in the corner like your typical pretty wallflower.

Then she told herself that she'd have her boyfriend, Eric, to talk to, but even that didn't make her feel like going out tonight. Maybe her melancholy mood could be chalked up to a bad case of PMS, or maybe it was because she was a few days shy of getting her last report card for the year. That always made her nervous, even though she usually did just fine. Maybe it was because she worried her chronic shyness was going to get the better of her once again. Whatever the reason, she looked at Larissa as she got all dolled up and hoped her friend would break one of her well-manicured, Hard Candy–painted nails. Beauty crises had derailed their plans many, *many* times before, so why not now?

"If this shirt doesn't get me groped at least once tonight, I'm suing the designer." Larissa tugged at the straps of a rainbow-striped terry cloth tank so that it draped lower on her chest. She posed in front of the mirror hanging from the door of Cassidy's walk-in closet, flinging her long, straight hair behind her shoulders. She'd recently added bold red streaks, and they glinted in the late afternoon sunlight streaming through Cassidy's picture window.

"Larissa," Cassidy reminded her, "you *are* the designer."

"Too true," Larissa agreed. "What do you think? Will it be a hit on the runway?"

"You'll have Dior begging for mercy."

Cassidy rolled her eyes. Ever since Larissa had picked up an issue of *Nylon* magazine three months before, it was nearly impossible to tear her away from her sewing machine or get her to talk about anything besides cuts and fabrics. Larissa was convinced she was the next Coco Chanel, and Cassidy was waiting patiently for her to get over her fashion craze the way she'd gotten over rock climbing, karaoke, and synchronized swimming. They'd spent four summers together, and Cassidy just loved how Larissa's ever-so-fleeting passions always took them somewhere unexpected.

"Excellent. But if not," Larissa decided, "I'll give it to you."

"Thanks a million," she said acidly. "I'll wear it every day."

Cassidy knew that Larissa was well aware of the fact she wouldn't go anywhere near rainbow-striped terry cloth. She preferred simple, elegant clothes that made her blend in, not stand out. With her porcelain-colored skin, huge blue eyes, and endless lashes, she got enough attention as it was—too much, considering she was usually too timid to talk to any guys besides Eric. Even so, she still got tongue-tied around him, and they had been dating for almost two years.

Wow, has it really been that *long?* she thought.

"Look, a little color won't kill you." Larissa sighed, taking in Cassidy's black crepe button-down shirt from Theory, plain white flip-flops, and short denim skirt. "Come on, I've got this new eye shadow that would look amazing on you. It's hardly a color at all. Actually, it's more of a subtle shimmer. . . ."

Larissa began rummaging in the enormous straw tote she carried everywhere she went. Cassidy giggled to herself, picturing the mess of makeup, loose change, and empty Twizzler wrappers lurking in the bottom. She imagined the bag swallowing Larissa whole, so that only her newly painted lime green toenails stuck out from the top.

The image was too good to pass up. She grabbed her sketchbook off the nightstand and began covering a page in small, quick lines. As she drew with her favorite Hello Kitty number-two pencil, she felt the tiny knot she always carried around inside her begin to loosen. Secretly, she called it "social tension"—the feeling of always having to say something and never knowing what to say, so that she ended up just not talking and seeming stuck-up to everyone but her closest friends. Drawing was always good for that. It let her enter a silent world where she could sit back and watch without having to say anything at all.

In fact, the walls of Cassidy's room were covered in her sketches: Larissa morphing into Kelly Clarkson as she belted into the mike of a karaoke machine, Eric riding a horse backward along Zuma Beach, and all three of them playing tug-of-war with a giant Twizzler.

Her favorite, which she'd tinted with colored pens and hung prominently over her bed, showed Larissa as Batman and her as Robin, both poised to leap off the roof of their high school and save the desperately bored students trapped inside. It seemed to sum up their friendship perfectly: the way outgoing, talkative Larissa always took the lead and quiet Cassidy was content to play sidekick. Some girls might not have been into playing Haley James to Larissa's Peyton Sawyer, but Cassidy found it comforting. She didn't want the limelight and liked that Larissa was always thinking of new fun things for them to do. As far as she was concerned, they complemented each other perfectly. Besides, she knew Larissa wouldn't be so gutsy without Cassidy's support—and if it weren't for Larissa, Cassidy would probably forget how to talk entirely.

"Are you cartooning me again?" Larissa asked, breaking Cassidy's concentration so that her head jerked up, sending her hand skittering across the page.

Larissa leaned over to examine the new sketch. "My bag is eating me!" she exclaimed.

Cassidy nodded and grinned.

"When I'm a famous designer, I'll have to get you to do my sketches," Larissa said. "You're the one with all the artistic talent. All I have is the vision. Don't you think we'll make a great team?"

"Haven't we always?" Cassidy asked.

Larissa smiled conspiratorially. "It's almost like we share a brain. Which is good because mine seems to be missing half the time anyway. So are you going to let me put this eye shadow on you or what?"

"Can you at least tell me what color it is?" Cassidy asked. "I don't trust your definition of 'light shimmer.'"

"I told you this will look amazing. Trust me."

"I don't know." Cassidy hesitated. "Eric's really not into heavy makeup."

"No offense, but Eric's not exactly the next Armani," Larissa said. "I think he's worn the same pair of Diesel jeans every day since 2002. Come on, Cass. Live a little."

Cassidy sighed and closed her eyes. When Larissa put her mind to something, it was hard to stop her. She felt something cool and sticky settling on her eyelids and breath tickling her forehead.

"Voilà!" Larissa shouted. Cassidy opened her eyes. Her friend was smirking as if she'd just done something blue ribbon–worthy. "If I were a guy, I would totally do you."

Cassidy got up to check herself out in the mirror. The girl staring back at her was definitely still Cassidy: a petite five-foot-five, with a thick cloud of deep brown hair curled gently around her high cheekbones and small, pointed chin. But then there were the green rings surrounding her light blue eyes. It was "shimmering," all right. The metallic gleam practically made her look radioactive.

"Larissa!" Cassidy wailed. "I look like a Powerpuff Girl!"

"Oh, please," grumbled Larissa. "You look fantastic. We have to get you over your fear of color this summer if we're both going to work at Seersucker."

The week before, Larissa had dragged her into a new boutique in downtown Malibu to ask for summer jobs. The owners, two recent fashion-school grads with blunt bangs and lots of earrings, had hired them on the spot. Whether they'd been charmed by Larissa's personality and Cassidy's shy smile or just happy to get cheap high-school labor was anyone's guess.

"Well, if it comes down to it, maybe I'll wear some red lipstick or something," Cassidy mused.

"I'll believe it when I see it." Larissa snorted.

Through her open window, Cassidy heard the familiar blare of 50 Cent with too much bass and gravel crunching in the driveway.

"Sounds like Eric's here," she said, an unstoppable grin spreading across her face.

"I'm surprised he can hear anything that registers under two thousand decibels," Larissa joked.

Cassidy heard the front door slam shut in the big

marble foyer and Eric's footsteps bounding up the stairs. The door to Cassidy's room swung open and her boyfriend stepped inside, all six feet of him.

"What, no knock?" Larissa scolded. "We could have been indecent, you know."

"You're always indecent, Larissa," Eric joked, sweeping Cassidy into his arms so that her feet came off the floor.

He had been surfing again at Point Dume. She could smell the salt on his neck and the scent of his Banana Boat SPF 4 sunblock. His curly black hair was slightly damp too. He spun her around and gave her a noisy smack on the lips before gently putting her down again.

Cassidy gazed at Eric's deep Dominican tan and the way the skin around his eyes crinkled from sun and laughter. She loved Eric: everyone did. Even her parents were charmed by him and they were picky about *everything*.

Eric was squinting down at her. "Sweetie, what's up with your eyes?" he asked. "You look like a Powerpuff Girl."

Larissa laughed heartily. "Jeez, Cass. I thought I was the only one you shared your brain with."

Cassidy began to blush as she fumbled on her vanity table for a cleansing pad. "I forgot I even had it on."

Eric chuckled. "You're so beautiful, you don't need that stuff."

"Dude!" Larissa cried. "I walk around with half of

Sephora's inventory on my face. Does that mean I'm busted or something?"

Eric quickly changed the subject. "Where's the party tonight?"

"Near Pepperdine," Larissa answered. "Sig Ep is having an end-of-the-year bash. I heard they always burn the furniture that nobody's taking home, so it should get pretty wild."

"I'm always down for a good fire." He put his arm around Cassidy, and she snuggled into his chest. "Are you up for it, hon?"

Cassidy loved how he was always looking out for her. She kissed his lips gingerly in thanks. "Now I am."

"Um, *puke*," Larissa said. "Shouldn't you two get a room or something?"

"This *is* my room," Cassidy reminded her.

"Oh yeah." Larissa shrugged. "So, like, is your mom home or what?"

"No, she's at Lea Eigard learning some facial exercises or something," Cassidy said. "You can go try on her shoes. I won't tell."

"Score!" Larissa said, winking at Eric before leaving the room, pointedly closing the door behind her.

As soon as she was gone, Eric picked Cassidy up and carried her to the bed, setting her down gently on top of the covers. "I'm glad we're getting a couple of minutes alone," he said.

Then Eric lay next to her, stretching his arm out so she could rest her head in the hollow between his chest and shoulder. Snuggling into him and smelling the faint trace of sweat under the sheen of saltwater coating his skin, Cassidy sighed with contentment. Nobody made her feel quite as comfortable or secure as Eric: Ever since he'd asked to borrow the bottle of soy sauce on her table at Nobu two summers ago, she'd been hooked on his loose laugh and sexy brown eyes.

Eric craned his head to kiss her lightly on the mouth. His was warm and as sweet as buttered popcorn. Cassidy let the kiss go on, closing her eyes as Eric's body rubbed against hers and thinking how lucky she was to have such a fine boyfriend. Under her hand, which had crept beneath his shirt, the skin on his chest was smooth and taut. She heard a breath catch in his throat as his hand engulfed hers, gently guiding it toward his stomach and then lower.

Even more gently, Cassidy pulled her hand away.

"Larissa's waiting for us," she reminded him.

"Larissa's looking at shoes," Eric said, eyes half-closed. A smile twitched at the corners of his mouth. "Time ceases to exist when girls are around shoes."

Cassidy laughed and planted a light kiss on his lips. He grabbed her, massaging her shoulders with deep, strong strokes as his tongue found its way inside her mouth again. She felt her body arching against his in spite of herself. But once again, she made herself stop before things got too heavy.

"You don't want to get to the party after the keg runs out, do you?" she teased, sitting up and smoothing her hair. She could feel her cheeks burning where Eric's stubble had rubbed against them.

"It wouldn't be the end of the world," Eric said.

Cassidy squeezed his hand. It wasn't that she didn't want to go all the way with Eric. Who wouldn't? He was practically the finest-looking guy at Malibu High, and she was lucky to have him. But there was something that hadn't been established, and Cassidy could only hand over her virginity with a clear conscience.

She swallowed hard. "Hey, can I ask you a silly question?"

Eric nodded, and she took a deep breath and forced herself to look him in the eye. "How do you feel about me?"

His forehead crinkled with confusion. "What do you mean, how do I feel about you?" he asked. "You're my girlfriend. I'm crazy about you. You know that."

"Yeah," Cassidy said. "I guess I do."

Eric continued to squint down at her. "Why?" he asked. "How do you feel about *me*?"

"Oh," Cassidy said. "I . . ."

The words stuck in her throat. There was no way

she could say "I love you" to Eric before he said it to her. Every article in the women's magazines she and Larissa liked to giggle over insisted that saying it first was relationship suicide. But after nearly two years of dating, shouldn't it be out in the open? She was almost positive that Eric *did* love her, but there was no way she was going to risk letting the words slip without *knowing* first.

"I'm crazy about you too," she finished softly.

"Good." Eric's face relaxed into a grin and he leaned forward, kissing her again. Cassidy counted to ten in her head before putting her hands on his shoulders and pushing him away.

"We should get going," she said. "Really."

"Okay." Eric sighed, not meeting her eyes as he climbed off the bed.

He was too nice a guy to say anything, but Cassidy could tell he was annoyed she had never let him take things all the way. As close as she felt to Eric, Cassidy could never in a million years tell him that the "I love you" factor was keeping them from having sex. She knew it was silly and old-fashioned and really just a formality, but she still wanted to hear it, and was positive that as soon as the words were out of his mouth, she'd be rushing to Victoria's Secret to buy the laciest thong she could find.

"Let's go, gorgeous," Eric said, finally meeting her

eyes and smiling so that the comma-shaped dimple on his left cheek seemed to dance.

Cassidy smiled back at him. She grabbed her purse in one hand and Eric's arm in the other and wondered what was to come in the night ahead.

Chapter Two

few hours later, Cassidy was being crushed by a swarm of sticky, perspiration-soaked, barely clothed bodies. To her left were guys in white baseball hats, punching each other on the arm and calling each other "bro." To her right were Tara Reid clones comparing tans and belly button rings and asking if there was any diet tonic left to mix with the vodka. Pepperdine's Sigma Phi Epsilon fraternity was notorious for debauchery, and Cassidy could see why. A lot of people were already grinding their pelvises on the dance floor in the living room or funneling a variety of alcoholic beverages in the kitchen. As for Eric, he'd disappeared five minutes before to fill up their plastic cups with more Coors Light, which left Cassidy alone with Larissa, the boy-guzzling machine.

"Holy crap." Larissa grabbed Cassidy's arm suddenly in a death grip. "Look at that guy over there. I think I'm going to melt, he's so hot."

Cassidy followed Larissa's gaze to a thin guy with lanky blond hair and an enormous nose.

"Are you sure?" Cassidy asked. "What about that thing in the middle of his face?"

"Face?" Larissa asked, bewildered. "Honey, check out his *shoes*." Cassidy looked down. The guy had on a gorgeous pair of gray suede Gucci loafers, which looked great under a faded pair of Lucky jeans.

"Let's go talk to him before he watches too many *Queer Eye* episodes and decides to go home and re-upholster his sofa or something."

Cassidy tried peering over the crowd to find Eric, but before she knew it, Larissa's hand was in hers and they were both surging through the crowd, hot on the trail of Gucci Boy.

"You better watch out," Larissa warned him when they emerged safely on the other side of the mob. "I heard there's a plot under way to get you drunk and steal your shoes."

Startled at first, he broke into a huge grin at the sight of the two girls. Nose and all, Cassidy had to admit that when he smiled, he *was* kind of cute. She could sense Larissa sneaking glances at her, trying to gauge her approval, and gave her a barely perceptible nod.

"I think I can fend for myself," he said, grinning. "Believe it or not, I actually *do* work out once in a while."

"I wouldn't doubt it for a moment," Larissa said. "So what's your name?"

"Can you guess?" He wiggled his eyebrows suggestively.

"I dunno. Maybe a Dan? Sergio? Harry?" Larissa asked.

"You're about as wrong as you can be." He laughed, extending his hand. "I'm Jay."

Larissa took his hand, letting her palm linger just a tad longer than necessary as she introduced herself. "I never would have guessed," she purred. "I'm Larissa. And this is Cassidy, my bestest friend for life."

Jay smiled. "Nice to meet you, Bestest Friend for Life."

Cassidy withdrew her hand after something like half a pump and immediately felt silly. What did she think, he was going to *eat* her or something? She was always such a wreck when it came to talking with strangers. Even when Eric had approached her at Nobu, she'd been so anxious when she'd handed him the soy sauce that she'd dropped it on his foot. He'd been wearing Tevas and his big toe immediately had begun to swell up. He'd pressured her into giving her his number so that his "lawyer" could call her. It was so sweet.

"Nice to meet you, um, Not Sergio," she said, realizing as soon as the words were out of her mouth that she sounded like a moron. The pressure of small talk just *did* that to her sometimes. She tried to be funny, and then it became obvious to everyone how awkward she was.

But Jay didn't seem to have even heard her. "So you girls go to Pepperdine?" He casually glanced at the way the strap of Larissa's tank top had slipped off her shoulder.

"No, we just hang around campus hoping to meet guys like you," Larissa quipped.

"You don't want to meet guys like *him*," interjected a guy with black hair gelled up into tiny spikes. "He's trouble. Not like me. I'm a *nice* guy."

"Oh, but nice guys are no fun!" Larissa said.

Cassidy could tell Larissa loved all the attention, and this was why hanging out with her made Cassidy kind of depressed. She didn't begrudge Larissa's talent for flirting or how easily her best friend turned a boring conversation into a laugh-fest. She didn't aspire to *be* Larissa either. She just envied how Larissa was so comfortable with being herself and letting other people get to know exactly who she was. Cassidy had never really been able to fully do that, even with Eric. She still felt like even though he had been holding back those three little words, there was much more that she was holding back from him and from everyone else she knew. Cassidy wished she could find out the secret to unlocking the interesting, engaging person that always seemed to show up in her sketches. She knew she wasn't going to find out what it was tonight, so she drew in a large breath and decided it was time to sink or swim.

"Eric is nice and fun," Cassidy interjected automatically. "And Dominican."

Oh my God, why am I even talking? she thought.

"Who's Eric?" asked Jay.

"He's, um—a surfer," Cassidy stammered, barely managing to get the words out of her mouth. *Duh! That's not all he is.* "And he's my boyfriend," she added nervously.

"Oh, you guys have boyfriends?" Jay looked disappointed.

"*She* does." Larissa's eyes flashed Cassidy a tiny warning. "I, on the other hand, am delightfully single. Who wants to be my date tonight?" She crooked her elbow in invitation and the two guys nearly collided with each other trying to grab it first.

Cassidy panicked at the thought of having to come up with more things to say to these guys, so she did what any self-respecting shy person would do—run fast and far, far away.

"I think I'm going to find the ladies' room," she whispered to Larissa.

"You sure?"

"I'll be fine," Cassidy assured her. All she wanted was

to go somewhere quiet where she could get her bearings and plan out her next conversation—word for word.

* * *

The line for the bathroom snaked through the kitchen and into the hall. Great. En route to the one place at the party where she could be alone, Cassidy was surrounded.

"My, oh my, Miss Cassidy Jones."

The voice came from behind her. She spun around.

With his dyed blond hair and his signature scrubby jeans (complete with a tear in the crotch), Joe Telesky usually looked like he'd just rolled out of bed. But Cassidy knew that in her mind, he'd always be the kid down the block who used to spend his summers making a bunch of noise while erecting his state-of-the-art tree house. Cassidy and Joe were neighborhood pals during the BE period—Before Eric. From sixth grade until freshman year of high school, Cassidy had gone to Joe's special fortress to play Pictionary, which was how he'd originally lured her off her front porch. But once she'd gotten a serious boyfriend and begun hanging out with Larissa more, Joe had morphed from a childhood buddy into a classroom acquaintance. Still, whenever they did run into each other, it was like seeing a favorite cousin at a family reunion.

Cassidy put her arms around Joe and gave him a big

hug. He was so wiry and skinny that when she squeezed him tight, he actually let out a gasp of air. And he smelled like turpentine—Joe pretty much lived in his father's garage, which doubled as a workshop. He built everything from the desk in his room to the bookshelves in his parents' den. He'd even made an easel for Cassidy in honor of her fourteenth birthday. That was two years ago, and it was the last time they'd really hung out. Now that she was right in front of Joe's kind, Adam Brody–esque face, she felt a pang of regret about not staying in better touch with him.

"How have you been?" she asked. "I feel like I haven't seen you in forever."

"They don't call me J-Low Profile for nothing," Joe reminded her. "What are you doing here?"

"Larissa and Eric brought me," she replied.

Joe chuckled. "You mean dragged you!"

Cassidy blushed. Joe really did know the score. "Kind of."

"Heading to the bathroom for cover?" Joe laughed.

"No, I–I was just . . ." Cassidy stammered. "Trying to find the keg."

"Such a party animal," he said with a grin. "Come on, I'll show you a shortcut. There's one upstairs that's probably easier to get into than a White Stripes concert."

"Sounds good," Cassidy said. Hanging out with Joe was definitely better than brooding in a corner by herself.

She followed him into the kitchen, where he opened a door that she could have sworn belonged to a closet. Behind it was a flight of rickety wooden stairs.

"Servants quarters," Joe explained. "These houses used to belong to ritzy families. They'd probably be rolling over in their graves if they knew what was going on here today."

"Since when did you become such an expert?"

"Scotto is king of the Frat Monkeys," Joe explained. "Don't tell him I called them monkeys, though. He'll kick my ass."

Cassidy giggled. "I won't. Promise."

"There's a mini-keg in here," he said, knocking on a door covered in a ripped batik tapestry. "Better beer. It's supposed to just be for the frat brothers, but I'm real family."

"Who is it?" a voice boomed from inside.

"Your brother," Joe called back. "And guest."

"Male or female?"

Joe rolled his eyes at Cassidy. "Female," he said. "But hands off. She's very taken. A buff surfer would end you if you did anything stupid."

"Fine," was the final verdict. "Come on in."

Joe led Cassidy into a room so smoky it took several moments for her eyes to penetrate the haze. She tried not to cough as Joe introduced her to a cadre of frat brothers huddled around a glass-topped coffee table littered with ashtrays, empty beer cans, and copies of *Scientific American* and *Maxim* magazine. The glass bong sitting in the middle was almost taller than she was.

She couldn't catch any of the names except for Scotto, Joe's brother, who looked like an older, chunkier version of Joe. He was wearing purple sweatpants and a T-shirt that had the *Onion* logo splashed across the front and was sitting cross-legged on an armchair without any legs.

"Welcome!" Scotto bellowed. "And what can I offer you this fine evening? I've got Blue Hawaiian, this great hydro from Humboldt, and I think there's Vicodin around here somewhere. . . ."

"Actually, we kind of just want some beer," Joe said.

Scotto waved his hand. "Whatever, man."

Joe fished two red plastic cups out of a paper bag and poured them both beers from the keg. Cassidy took a sip of hers. It was cool and bitter. She hadn't realized how thirsty she was.

"Who wants to smoke?" Scotto asked abruptly.

All the hands in the room went up except for Joe's and Cassidy's.

"Excellent." Scotto fished several plastic baggies from under the cushion of his seat.

"We have to get going," Joe said.

Scotto looked genuinely hurt. "So soon?"

"Yeah, I think there's a chugging contest brewing

downstairs and Cassidy's favored three to one." Joe reached out and tousled his brother's hair.

"Wow, awesome," Scotto said. "Well, can you do me a favor?"

Joe nodded.

Scotto found a plastic baggie under his seat cushion. This one was labeled PURPLE HAZE. "Can you take this down to Jordan? I promised him a sample."

Joe pocketed the bag. "No problem, bro," he said. "See you later."

"Wow," Cassidy said when they were out the door. "Your brother—"

"Smokes more dope than the kids on *That '70s Show*," Joe said. "Yeah, I know. My parents made him take the LSAT his junior year of college just to see how he'd do, and he aced it without even having to study. But he can't seem to get it together enough to graduate . . . after seven years."

Cassidy's head already felt a little lighter and she was loosening up. Not as much as Scotto, but enough that she wasn't nearly as worried about having to talk to people she didn't know.

Joe and Cassidy walked out to the backyard, where there was a DJ booth and a fire ring that had been cleared and edged with stones. Cassidy breathed deeply, letting the cool, damp summer air invade her lungs, glad to be free of the suffocating beery smokiness inside the frat house.

"Do they really burn all the furniture that nobody wants?" she asked.

"The Sig Eps have a very unique philosophy," Joe replied. "If you don't like a particular piece, even if it's not yours, you can burn it. And if you *do* like one that's somebody else's, you can steal it from them. Of course, they can steal it back from you as well, but that's part of the fun. So around this time of year, there's a lot of bartering and stealing going on, and you have to be pretty vigilant to keep something you really like from going up in flames."

Cassidy couldn't help laughing. "That's ridiculous."

"There was one guy who strapped his favorite chair to his back and walked around like that for weeks before the end-of-year party. At night, he'd padlock it to the post of his bed."

"Did it work?" Cassidy giggled.

"No," Joe admitted. "They dismantled his bed while he was sleeping and hid the piece with his chair attached in another frat house. He was inconsolable. In fact, that's him over there." He pointed to a stocky guy in a green knit cap sitting by himself in the corner, drinking a beer and staring up at the stars with a "Why me?" expression on his face.

"Poor man," Cassidy said. "Should we go cheer him up?"

Joe shook his head. "I've tried," he said. "We all have. They even gave him back his chair when they realized the deeper psychological impact. But I don't think that was it. I think it was just having his plan thwarted. It insulted his intelligence."

"The complexity of the male psyche," Cassidy agreed. "Who knows its bounds? It's like boys have all these weird secrets I'll never understand."

"Boys?" Joe asked. "What about the girls? They're the ones with the weird secrets. At least, they always manage to confuse *me*."

"I guess you're right," Cassidy said. "I mean, I *am* a girl, and half the time I can't even understand what's going on in my *own* head."

"Hey, isn't that your boyfriend?"

Cassidy's eyes followed his. Sure enough, Eric was coming through the crowd of dancers, a beer balanced in each hand. His eyes lit up when he saw her but clouded slightly when he noticed Joe.

"Hey, sweetie," he said, leaning down for a kiss. Cassidy noticed Joe's grin falter out of the corner of her eye. "I've been looking all over for you. Where've you been?"

"Oh, Joe was just showing me around," she said. "You guys know each other, right?"

"Yeah, sure," Eric said.

"How's it going?" Joe asked, reaching out to shake Eric's hand. But Eric was too busy wrapping his arm around Cassidy's shoulders to notice.

"So I brought you a drink," he said, squeezing her tight. "But it looks like you already have one."

"That's okay; I can finish it quick," Cassidy said. She tipped her head back and let the rest of the beer slide down her throat. Her cup had been about halfway full, and a tiny trickle spilled down her chin when she reached the bottom. She righted her head, wiped her chin, and hiccupped.

"Now I can have this one," she said, reaching for the cup in Eric's hand.

"Maybe you should take a little break first," Joe warned. "I could get you a glass of water or something."

"She'll be fine," Eric assured him coolly, then turned to Cassidy. "They're about to start the bonfire. Let's go find a good spot."

"Where's Larissa?" Cassidy asked. The thought of her current best friend and her old best friend hooking up suddenly seemed like a great idea. Maybe the beer was drowning the neurons in her brain.

"I think I saw her making out with someone in the kiddie pool," Joe said.

So much for that, she thought.

Eric tugged on her arm a little. "Come on, we don't want to miss the first futon in the fire pit."

Cassidy glanced over at Joe, who was looking a little dejected. He put his hands in his pockets and leaned back on his heels as if he were trying to plan his exit.

Cassidy felt kind of bad that Eric wasn't being friendlier to him. It was unusual, actually. She rarely saw Eric be anything but warm and jovial.

"I'm probably going to head out," Joe mumbled.

Cassidy frowned. "Not yet. You'll miss the bonfire."

"It'll never match the first time I saw jocks douse a bunch of stuff in lighter fluid, though," Joe joked. "Why put myself through the disappointment?"

Eric barely cracked a smile. "See you later." Then he tugged on Cassidy's arm harder and pulled her away before she could even say good-bye.

As they stood in front of the crowd that gathered near the fire ring, Cassidy felt a surge of annoyance rise in her. Why was Eric being so pushy and weird? And where on earth was Larissa? She was the person who had orchestrated this whole evening and she had abandoned Cassidy to go off somewhere and get it on with God knows who. Then there was Joe. She was having a nice time with him, just like she always had, but now she was sure that he thought she was a loser for allowing Eric to pull her away.

Soon a ruckus emerged from inside the house. A large group of husky guys began dragging furniture out into the backyard. The crowd chanted, "Chet! Chet! Chet!" as a burly boy poured something that smelled like gasoline onto what looked like a Pier 1 Papasan chair. Within seconds, Cassidy felt the heat from four-foot crackling flames on her skin and heard Eric and everyone else yelping for joy.

She wished she could be more excited. Summer was practically here. That's what this celebration was all about. But Cassidy couldn't muster up enough enthusiasm to cheer with her fellow partygoers. All she did was think about how she would sketch this moment—and that the only color she would use was gray.

Chapter Three

From: Larissaland@gmail.com
Sent: Wednesday, June 14
To: Cassidy.Jones@gmail.com
Re: Seersuckaaaaaaaaaaaaaa!!!!

Dude C, I am so psyched about our summer jobz!
Talked 2 Fumiko & she said we'll be working 9–5
m–f for $11/hour + we get a 30% discount =
sweet! My ass will be the best dressed in Malibu
this summer. No, not Nicole Richie—me!
So psyched. Can't wait. So psyched. Can't wait.

xoxoxoxoxoxoxoxo,
L

Even though she'd drawn her window shades as tight as they would go, bright yellow sunlight still filtered into Cassidy's room around their edges, ruining the calming effect of her favorite blue lightbulb. She really should have avoided those farewell Jell-O shots at the party the night before. They'd already ruined what was supposed to be a beautiful Saturday at Zuma Beach with Eric. After hiding under a floppy sun hat and rubbing her temples all afternoon, she had finally begged off to go home and chill with a Norah Jones CD and her sketchbook. She was trying to draw the gnomes inside her head, who were bashing away at her skull with their tiny gnome hammers.

She was so wrapped up in sketching that she didn't get up to answer her cell until the third ring.

"Cassidy," her mother's voice came leaping through the receiver. "Did you forget we had scheduled dinner tonight?"

"Of course not," Cassidy lied. "I was just on my way down."

She could hear the phone snap shut on the other end of the line. As an efficiency expert, her mom didn't believe in saying good-bye to someone she was going to see again in five minutes. She also believed in scheduling family dinners two to three times a week to "promote closeness and communication," as she wrote in her best-selling self-help book *All the Time in the World*.

Cassidy glanced quickly at herself in the mirror and ran a brush through her hair. "Respect Your Appearance, Respect Yourself" was her favorite chapter in her mother's book. Sandra Jones liked her family to practice what she preached.

Dinner was already on the table as Cassidy hopped off the bottom step. She glanced guiltily at the words FAMILY DINNER written prominently in the seven o'clock time slot on the erasable whiteboard hanging in the front hall. It was unlike her to forget things like that. In fact, she usually set the alarm on her cell phone to go off a few minutes beforehand so she could be down in time to help her mother get dinner on the table.

Cassidy took her usual spot at one end of the long glass-and-marble dining room table, next to her dad and across from her mom. Her mouth watered as she eyed the chicken roasted with rosemary until the skin was crisp and the inside juicy and sweet, potatoes mashed with just the right amount of butter, and string beans steamed so they still crunched when you bit into them. There were fresh tiger lilies in a hand-blown glass vase on the table, and quiet classical music played in the background. "If You're Gonna Take the Time to Do Something, You Might as Well Do It Right" was another chapter in Mom's book.

But tonight something was different. Her parents seemed tense with excitement, like they had a big, wonderful secret hanging in the air between them. It buzzed around her mom's carefully styled dark hair and coral-colored Chanel lipstick and seemed to bounce off the paunch sticking out from her father's argyle sweater vest.

"So Cassidy," her mother said, smiling as she squeezed a wedge of lime into her club soda. "According to my calendar, school is almost out for the year."

"Yeah, it is," Cassidy agreed. "Just finals on Monday and Tuesday, Wednesday to pick classes for next year, clean out our lockers on Friday, and then I'm free."

"And how do you expect to do on finals?" Sandra probed. "I know we were looking at mostly A's during midterms."

"I've been studying real hard," Cassidy replied. "I even joined a study group for American history." She didn't mention that the study group consisted of her, Larissa, and two girls who were perpetually sneaking out of the library to smoke cigarettes behind the Dumpsters, and that they mostly talked about which *American Idol* contestants had the worst hair. "Always Stress the Positive" was yet another chapter in her mom's book, and Cassidy had memorized every line in it.

"And how about French?" Sandra asked. Cassidy noticed that even though her mother had peeled the skin off her chicken breast, none of the food had actually made it to her mouth.

"I should do just fine," she said. "I've gotten A's on all

the quizzes so far." All the written quizzes, at least. Cassidy decided to leave out Monsieur Stuart's displeasure at her refusal to speak in class. She wasn't a conversationalist in her native language. How did the man expect her to start yapping it up in one that she barely understood?

"Excellent." Cassidy watched her parents exchange glances. Something was *definitely* up. "Because we have some good news for you."

"Great news," Laurent Jones agreed, his mustache twitching with anticipation.

"Really?" Cassidy's mind reeled with possibilities. Maybe they'd decided that if she got an A in every subject, she would get a Lexus or something. She hated driving her mom's Volvo; it had *middle-aged self-help writer* written all over it.

"Yes," her mom continued. "We've enrolled you in a wonderful summer program. Only the best students are accepted."

"Summer . . . program?" Maybe she'd heard wrong. It wouldn't be unlikely, considering the way the gnomes were still hammering away at her head.

"I'm so glad to hear you're doing well in French because you'll be taking an accelerated French course at Pepperdine. You know what that means, right?"

"No," Cassidy croaked. She took a long gulp of water, hoping it would make her throat feel less tight and dry. But it didn't.

"It means you can stay with Aunt Geraldine in Paris when you study abroad your junior year of college," her mother crowed. "Won't that be nice?"

"But . . . college is like a million years away," Cassidy said, confused.

"College will be here before you know it," her mother said, her smile faltering for a moment. "And what have I always taught you about thinking ahead?"

"It's never too early." Cassidy sighed.

"That's right. This way, you can take AP French in school next year and be nearly fluent by the time you're in college. Then when it's time to live in France, you'll be speaking like a native. Won't that be perfect?"

Perfect? Cassidy stared at her mom, openmouthed with confusion. How could anyone possibly think being locked in a stuffy classroom all day was *perfect?* Didn't she understand that the whole point of summer was not having to smell chalk dust and worry about homework assignments for almost three whole months? She realized she was stirring her mashed potatoes violently and looked up to see her parents staring at her expectantly, ready for her to thank them so they could break into exultant smiles.

"Actually, I already made plans for the summer." Cassidy strove to sound chipper and upbeat. "Larissa and I both got jobs at Seersucker."

"Seer-*what?*" her mother asked, incredulous.

Cassidy's resolve was already beginning to falter. "It's this really cool new clothing boutique downtown."

"You can do retail any old summer. If you even want to, that is," she said firmly. "This is the chance of a lifetime, Cassidy. Do you have any idea how competitive this program is? Only one in four students gets in, and we had to submit your PSAT scores and transcripts from the last two years. We knew it was a gamble, so we didn't want to tell you in case you didn't make the cut. See how enriching this looks?" Her mother pushed a glossy folder across the tabletop toward her daughter. Even for an announcement over a family meal, Sandra Jones had brought visual aids.

There was a photo collage on the front: snapshots of smiling students strolling across the Pepperdine quad and posing for pictures in front of the Eiffel Tower. CALIFORNIA INTERNATIONAL LANGUAGE AND CULTURE INSTITUTE was embossed across the top.

"We're so excited for you," her father added in his gentle accent. "You know how much it bothers me that I had to give up my cultural roots when I came to America to marry your mom. And it's just a shame that you never really got to know my side of the family. This will . . . this will . . ." He struggled for the right word. He was an engineer and, like Cassidy, more comfortable drawing lines on paper than talking.

"This will *facilitate communication* between you and

your French relatives," her mom finished for him. "And give your summer some structure, unlike last year."

Cassidy remembered CJLK, the electroclash girl band she and Larissa had started the summer before. They'd spent days on end in Cassidy's room trying on microminis, downloading Fischerspooner tunes, and scribbling lyrics about falling in love with your hairdresser, before Larissa decided that bands were out and slam poetry was actually the next big thing.

"But I *am* going to have structure," Cassidy pleaded, realizing she was dangerously close to whining. "I said I have a job."

Her mother made eye contact and held it for so long that Cassidy finally looked away. She stared down at her plate, knowing she had already lost. "Honey, you know I don't believe in telling you what to do. But as an efficiency expert *and* as your mother, I *strongly recommend* you participate in this program. Your father and I will be happy to continue providing you with spending money, and we'd also be willing to discuss extending your weekend curfew by a few hours. How does that sound?"

"I don't know," Cassidy stalled, even though she knew exactly what she'd end up doing. Her mother drove a hard bargain, and Cassidy didn't think she had what it took to put up a fight. She felt like she had last night when Eric had pulled her away from Joe and when Larissa had made her tag along to talk with Gucci Boy.

She felt pressured and intimidated and she couldn't find the courage within her to say no.

Cassidy sighed an inner sigh, the kind that only she could hear, and pasted what she hoped was a brave smile across her face. "Fine, I'll do it."

"Oh, good!" her mother exclaimed. "Because I've already put down the deposit. You'll just love it, Cassidy, you'll see. You'll have lots of fun, maybe make some new friends. And of course it won't look too shabby on your college applications, either."

"Of course." Cassidy's voice echoed in her ears. "There's always that."

The rest of dinner felt like it lasted about a century and a half, and as if some medieval torture device had been attached to Cassidy's body. As her parents babbled on about the "extraordinary" benefits of the summer French program, Cassidy had to struggle to hold back her tears. As lukewarm as she'd felt about working at Seersucker before, it suddenly seemed like she was missing out on the most thrilling job in the history of seasonal employment. Plus Larissa would be crushed. They always did everything together.

And she hadn't even *begun* to think about Eric. He had a summer job lined up at Carl's Surf Shack, which meant he'd be at Point Dume all summer, teaching surfing lessons to adoring girls with skimpy Blink bikinis and killer Hawaiian Tropic tans while Cassidy languished in a classroom conjugating verbs with a bunch of type-A overachievers.

As soon as her mother got up to clear the plates, Cassidy excused herself. "I want some time to look this over," she said, patting the shiny folder and faking a smile.

"Sure, go ahead," her mom said as she and her father exchanged pleased glances. Cassidy could tell they considered the dinner a success. If only she could tell them how she really felt without bringing Armageddon down on her entire household.

The minute her bedroom door closed behind her, Cassidy threw herself facedown on her bed. She didn't *want* to cry about this like some big baby, but it was already too late. Streams of self-pity ran down her cheeks, and she dug her face into a pillow to drown out her sobs. It was just so unfair! Why had she ended up with parents so into planning her future that they forgot to notice how she felt in the present?

My summer is totally shot, Cassidy thought bitterly. With classes at 9 A.M. every morning, there was no way she'd be able to stay out late with Eric and Larissa like they'd planned. That was what summer was all about: long days at the beach, late nights driving around looking for trouble, waking up late the next morning and pouring yourself fresh-squeezed orange juice and starting all over again.

Without lifting her head from the pillow, Cassidy

fumbled on top of her nightstand for her cell phone and speed-dialed Larissa's number.

"Help . . ." was all she got out before choking on another sob.

"Bella's," Larissa commanded. "Ten minutes. See you there."

Cassidy clicked her phone shut and ran down the back stairs so her parents wouldn't see her puffy, tearstained face. She leapt into her mom's Volvo and started the engine, letting the wind from the open windows rush in to dry her tears. Tuning the radio to a bouncy Jason Mraz song, she cranked the volume and nodded to the beat. Larissa had been right to choose their favorite ice cream parlor for an emergency meeting spot—it overlooked the ocean too, so the view was spectacular. Even if a praline sundae and the roar of the waves didn't cheer her up, Larissa would think of something. She always did.

*   *   *

"So what happened?" Larissa plucked a candy-striped napkin from the dispenser on top of the ice cream counter and handed it to Cassidy so she could dry her eyes. "Did you get in a fight with Eric?"

Cassidy shook her head. "This is even worse, if you can believe it."

Larissa's eyes widened. "You killed someone!" she gasped. "And you want me to help you hide the body?"

Cassidy laughed in spite of herself. Larissa always managed to put her in a better mood.

"No, it's not quite that bad," she admitted. "It just . . . sucks is all."

"You need ice cream," Larissa observed. "ASAP."

"I really do." Cassidy ordered her favorite praline sundae from the pimply boy behind the counter. Even though she'd just finished dinner, she could feel her stomach rumbling in anticipation. What was it about tragedy that triggered such intense sugar cravings?

Once they were settled on a pair of high stools near the window that overlooked the water, Larissa began the inquisition. "Are you going to tell me what this gigantic tragedy is, or do I have to guess?"

Cassidy swallowed a huge glob of ice cream as if she were throwing back a shot of her father's Wild Turkey. "I have to go to summer school."

"Summer school!" Larissa screamed so loud Cassidy almost fell off her stool. "Why? You've never gotten anything lower than a B-plus in your life."

"I know," Cassidy said miserably. "That's the problem. It's summer school for smart kids. My parents want me to learn French so I can study abroad and live with Aunt Geraldine my junior year of college."

Larissa looked confused. "But that's like a million years away."

"That's what *I* said! Can you believe it? If they were any more anal retentive, we wouldn't need a bathroom."

"Ew." Larissa's nose wrinkled in disgust. "But seriously, Cass, what are you going to do? You didn't say yes, did you?"

Cassidy didn't know how to answer. Instead she took another big bite of ice cream and let the cool creamy texture fill her mouth so she wouldn't have to speak.

Larissa lightly slapped Cassidy's forehead in dismay. "You did!"

"Ouch!" she yelped.

"I can't believe you're still letting them walk all over you like that. You're old enough to drive, you should be old enough to stand up to them."

"I know," Cassidy said miserably. "But you've seen how they are."

"I do." Larissa sighed. "They can be tough. But don't worry, Cass, we'll figure something out."

"Yeah?" Cassidy tried not to feel cynical, but she knew she was already locked into French school. All she could do was make the best of it, she supposed.

"I promise," Larissa assured her. "They don't call me Ms. Resourceful for nothing."

"Who calls you Ms. Resourceful?" Cassidy asked.

"Well, our bosses, for one," Larissa began. "They

were all excited about this idea I had to . . . oh." Her eyes and mouth opened into three wide O's of shock. "Wait a minute," she said slowly. "This means you won't be working with me at Seersucker this summer, doesn't it?"

"It does," Cassidy said. "How much does that suck?"

"Oh, man," Larissa gasped, her hands flying to her mouth. "What am I going to tell Fumiko and Dina? I just talked to them today. They were so happy to have two people who they knew would get along. Now it's just me. Great, Cassidy . . . I'm already starting off on the wrong foot."

"Sorry," Cassidy said. "I wish there were something I could do about it. Maybe you can find someone else?" Just saying it made her stomach ache. *She* was supposed to be the one working next to Larissa all summer, not some nameless *someone else*.

"I don't want someone else." Larissa looked just as panicked. "You have to get out of it," she said firmly.

Cassidy shook her head. "I don't think there's any way," she said. "I wish there were."

"You can't do this to me, Cassidy!"

"What do you mean, I can't do this to *you*?" Cassidy asked.

"You can't just ditch me like this!" Larissa repeated. "What am I supposed to do?"

As much as she loved Larissa, Cassidy could feel her teeth clenching around the cold metal spoon with annoyance. Sure, it wasn't *Larissa's* fault Cassidy was being forced into a summer of French drudgery, but could she maybe offer some moral support regardless?

"It's not like I'm thrilled about this either," she said. "You know I'd much rather work at Seersucker with you."

"Shit." Larissa's head drooped into her open palms. "This is just great, Cassidy. Now they're going to have to find someone to replace you. Plus they'll be mad at me. This totally blows."

"I *know*," Cassidy repeated. She wished Larissa would stop looking out for number one and go back to playing the sympathetic best friend. She didn't mind that Larissa always made herself the center of attention, but now that Cassidy was in the throes of a crisis, she wanted support, not more bailing out. "Don't think I don't feel bad about it."

"Well, of course it's not your *fault*," Larissa conceded. She absentmindedly dug a Twizzler out of her bag, unwrapped it, and dipped it in her ice cream. "Although I *do* wish you would learn to stand up to your parents."

"Easier said than done," Cassidy replied darkly. "Besides, it's too late now. My mom already put down the deposit."

Larissa sighed. "Well, look on the bright side," said finally. "Maybe there will be cute French guys."

Cassidy couldn't help cracking a smile at her friend's

flakiness. "Why would French guys come to America to study French?"

"Oh yeah." Larissa giggled. "Well, if there *are* any, send them my way."

"And what would you do with a French guy?" Cassidy asked suspiciously.

"Oh, you know, French things . . ." Larissa said vaguely. "Like zip around in his Alfa Romeo and go to wine tastings. And of course he'll have a boat so we can take you and Eric sailing," she finished. "Oh, *mon Dieu— c'est romantique, mon amour.*"

"That's, like, the entire extent of your French vocabulary, isn't it?" Cassidy asked through her giggles.

Larissa pretended to look hurt. "Um, *bonjour,*" she added. "Croissant!"

Cassidy was laughing so hard she forgot to be depressed and didn't remember her problems again until she was back home, trying to sleep with the specter of a summer of misery looming closer and closer in her mind.

Chapter Four

Friday was the last day of school, and Cassidy was helping Larissa clean out her locker, which had to be the messiest in all of Malibu High.

"Holy crap," Larissa said, holding up an apple that looked like it had expired sometime back in the Pleistocene age. "Does this look like the principal or what?"

Cassidy cracked up. The wrinkled apple actually *did* kind of resemble Mrs. Lorimer if you looked at it from a certain angle. Still, she had better things to do than sit around staring at fruit all day. The sign on the bank across the street said it was a balmy eighty-two degrees, and she was anxious to get outside. After all, she'd be spending more than enough time in a classroom soon enough.

"Can you clean a little faster?" she asked Larissa. "I want to get out of here."

"But Cassidy," Larissa teased. "You *love* school. That's why you decided to go to it all summer."

Cassidy leaned back against a locker and crossed her arms.

"Okay, look, I'm hurrying." Larissa dumped an arm-load of loose-leaf paper into a plastic bag. "Go recycle this or something for me, okay? I should be done by the time you get back."

Cassidy took the bag and headed down the hall toward the recycling bins. When she got there, she noticed a familiar figure lobbing an empty Coke can into the paper bin.

"Hey, Joe," she said, picking up the can and handing it back to him. "Good toss, but you may want to check what you're shooting for first."

"Oh, hey, Cass." Joe smiled when he saw her, but he looked tired or maybe sad. His yellow Pacific Sunwear shirt seemed to sag off his shoulders as he tossed the empty Coke into the correct bin.

"Everything okay?" Cassidy asked. "You're not pissed at me for bailing on you at the party, are you?"

"No, it's not that," Joe said.

"What's wrong?" Cassidy asked. "I haven't seen you this down since Casper died." She got a little choked up when she thought of their sixth-grade rabbit. It was the first funeral she'd ever gone to.

"I'm just bummed," he said. "It's my last night in town and my best friend—make that *former* best friend—ditched me to go see that new horror movie."

Cassidy wrinkled her nose. "That one about the crazy puppeteer?" Eric was dying to see it too.

"Puppets can be *really* scary," Joe said, smiling for the first time. "I was always terrified of Miss Piggy. She had such a temper."

Cassidy's phone buzzed in her back pocket, interrupting her laughter. It was Eric, texting to see if she wanted to see the movie.

NOT REALLY, she texted back.

Her phone rang a moment later.

"Are you sure?" Eric asked. "I heard it's up for Best Movie. At the MTV Movie Awards."

"As prestigious as that sounds, I think I'll pass." Cassidy laughed. "Actually, you should go. I just ran into Joe and he doesn't want to see it either, so I can hang out with him."

"Are you sure?" Eric's voice was tinged with concern. "I could skip the movie if you want to do something else instead."

"That's cool. I'll catch up with you later."

"Okay . . ." Eric still seemed reluctant to get off the phone. "So what are you and Joe going to do, anyway?"

There was that strange suspiciousness again. Eric was being so inquisitive, and the tone in his voice was eerily overbearing. He never seemed to care this much what she was up to when she was hanging out with Larissa. It seemed like he had some problem with Joe, which was ridiculous. He was brother material, not stud material.

"Probably just chill at his place. I haven't seen his mom in forever, and if I remember right, she makes amazing brownies."

"Sounds cool," Eric said, relaxing at the mention of parental involvement. "I'll call you as soon as the movie's out, okay?"

"Great." Cassidy stayed on the line for a moment longer, half hoping for an accidental "love ya," but Eric just hung up. She shrugged and shut her phone, giving Joe the thumbs-up. "Hope it's okay that I invited myself over!"

"Hey, I'm glad," said Joe. "What about Larissa? Should we ask her to come along?"

Cassidy glanced over her shoulder and spied Larissa immersed in an outdated *InStyle* magazine, her mouth hanging open and her eyes fixated on the pages. Streams of paper were still pouring out of her locker.

"She'll be here all night," she replied. "Let's go."

* * *

The tree house was just as Cassidy had remembered it. She could still smell the pungent scent of the shellac

Joe's dad had used to seal the roof from rain, and the sample carpet squares from Home Depot they'd sat on to avoid getting splinters in their butts were still tacked to the floors. She remembered watching the shadows lengthen over his backyard as they made up "secrets" about their teachers and giggled over a hidden stash of junk food. And now here they were again, sitting Indian style on a square of faded maroon carpet, drinking birch beer and gorging themselves on Cadbury Creme Eggs, Lays salt-and-vinegar potato chips, and a big roll of Pillsbury raw cookie dough—their version of the four food groups.

"Slow down," Cassidy warned Joe as he shoved an entire chocolate egg into his mouth. "You're going to asphyxiate yourself on old Easter candy. That's an embarrassing way to die."

"I can't help it. This feels like my last meal," Joe admitted. "I don't think I'll get to eat any of this stuff again for a long time."

"Why?" Cassidy helped herself to a chip. "You said you were going away or something, right?"

"Yeah." Joe sighed deeply and produced a crumpled brochure from his pocket. "Here."

McCaine Institute for At-Risk Youth—Summer Venture, was printed the front. It had a picture of wholesome smiling kids doing trail work with snow-capped mountains in the background.

"You're at risk?" Cassidy asked. "For what?"

"For turning into a big burnout like my brother, apparently," Joe said. "You know that bag of weed he gave me to hand off to his friend? Well, I totally forgot about it and my mom found it in my pocket when she was doing laundry the other day. She and my dad flipped out. I guess they're scared of producing another wayward kid like my brother, so they want to get me straightened out ASAP."

"But you didn't even smoke any of it," she said. "Did you?"

"No," Joe replied. "To tell the truth, I've never taken a hit in my life. I'm about as into the idea of turning into my brother as my parents are. Then again, he used to lie about it all the time, so I guess they have trust issues."

"That sucks!" Cassidy couldn't believe this. Joe's summer was actually going to be even worse than hers. At least her parents didn't have her pegged as something she wasn't.

"Justice is blind." Joe shrugged.

"But that doesn't mean your parents should be too," Cassidy argued. "Did you even get a chance to defend yourself?"

"Not really. As soon as they saw that bag, I knew I was done for. They're shipping me out tomorrow."

"And I thought *I* had it bad." Cassidy said, launching

into a description of the summer French course as Joe sat back against the wall of the tree house, munching a chunk of dough and nodding sympathetically.

"I guess neither of us is getting the summer we want," he said when she was through.

"I guess not." Cassidy sighed. "But what can we do about it?"

"Nothing," Joe agreed. "But I know what I want to do *now*." He looked down at his lap and chuckled softly to himself. "You'll think it's really lame, though."

"I won't," she assured him. "I promise."

"Okay. I'll be right back." Joe scurried down the tree house ladder and returned a few moments later with a large box under his arm.

"Pictionary?" Cassidy shrieked, glancing at the box. "You're my hero!"

Joe smiled. "I remembered how much you loved this game when we were kids."

Cassidy rubbed her hands together in anticipation. "Oh, I'm going to wipe the floor with you. Just you wait."

"Feeling a little competitive, eh, Jones? That is unwise," Joe said in the tone of voice that could only be heard in the overdubbing of kung fu movies.

"Fine, you go first," she said. "Let's see what you've got, Picasso."

Joe plopped back down on the carpet and opened

the game box. He got out a pad of paper and a pencil, picked up the card and read the clue, then turned over the miniature hourglass filled with sand. Joe scribbled frantically on the piece of paper. Cassidy thought he'd drawn stick people, but she wasn't entirely sure. So she just began guessing.

"They're bullfighters!"

"What? No way!" Joe replied.

Cassidy saw that time was ticking away and looked again at Joe's sketch pad as he kept drawing. "Um . . . oh! Wait, I got it. It's a cockfight!"

Joe stared at her. "No one's fighting, Cassidy. Jesus."

"I'm just calling it like I see it."

"Then you need glasses."

Joe scribbled some more and Cassidy became more lost than ever. When the clock ran out, he tossed his pencil at her, but she ducked to get out of the way.

"Hey, that could have poked my eye out!"

"It's not like it would matter. You can't see anyway," he said, smirking.

"What were you drawing?"

Joe sighed in frustration. "It was a carnival."

Cassidy looked at him blankly.

"See? There's the Ferris wheel, and there's the roller coaster," he said while pointing to what looked like a bunch of wacky lines.

Just then they made direct eye contact and burst into

hysterics. Cassidy clutched the part of her stomach that was starting to ache from sugar overload and laughter.

"Oh my God, I wonder what Eric would say if he knew I spent my evening playing Pictionary?"

"He'd probably be relieved," Joe pointed out. "If I had a girlfriend and she was off with some other guy and it turned out they were just playing a board game, I'd be pretty happy about it."

"Oh, I'm sure Eric trusts me," Cassidy said. But she wasn't as sure as she used to be. She thought about how Eric's voice had sounded anxious when she told him she was going to hang out with Joe instead of joining him at the movies. It's like he was jealous or something.

"I'm not saying he doesn't," Joe said. "I mean, you're the kind of girl who could never tell a lie. And I don't mean that in a George Washington kind of way or anything. Just that you're, like, super-honest. But that doesn't mean he's not worried in some little part of his mind. Guys are just like that."

"Do you really think so?" Cassidy asked.

"Definitely." Joe nodded.

"Is that one of those secret guy things I just don't understand?"

"I guess."

"Boys are such a mystery," Cassidy mused. "Hey, Joe, now that I have you cornered, maybe you could explain all the secrets of boys to me before you go."

"Only if you explain the secrets of girls to *me*," Joe said. "Not that I'll need much to seduce the female drug addicts."

Cassidy swatted Joe on the arm playfully. "If you must know, I think girls just want to be told they're loved."

"Is that all?" Joe asked. "Yo, girls!" he shouted, leaning his head out the window of the tree house. "I love you!"

Cassidy laughed. "You know what I mean."

"Well, it was worth a shot." Joe shrugged. He peeked out the window again. "Hey, what's wrong? The girls should be flocking to me by now."

"Maybe if you were their boyfriend and you told them you loved them and you meant it, they would," Cassidy said.

Joe looked at her quizzically. "Why? Eric doesn't say he loves you?"

Cassidy realized she might have inadvertently taken the conversation to a place it shouldn't have gone.

"I'm sorry," Joe said quickly. "That's a really personal question. You don't have to answer it."

"No, it's okay," she said. This was something she never talked about with anyone, not even Larissa, but she suddenly felt like she had to get it off her chest. "Actually, he doesn't. And I wish he would. It would make a huge difference."

They sat for a moment, listening to crickets chirp in

the grass below. "You know," Joe said quietly, "he's probably just scared. That's one secret boys don't want to get out, but it's true. Maybe he's scared that if he acts that attached, he'll be hurt when he loses you."

"But he's not going to lose me," Cassidy protested.

"Then let him know that. Boys are more insecure than you think. I mean, you don't have to get down on your knees and pledge eternal fidelity or anything, but there are subtle ways of letting him know you're not going anywhere."

"Like what?" Cassidy asked.

Cassidy couldn't tell in the gathering warm Malibu twilight whether Joe was blushing or not.

"Well, see, that's the hard part," he said. "I mean, I've never personally had a really intense relationship, so maybe just like . . . I don't know, tell him you think he's hot or whatever. Anything, I guess, just as long as you mean it."

Cassidy's phone was buzzing in her pocket, and her head was buzzing too, thanks to one hell of a sugar-induced rush. "I hope that's Eric. Then I can try your advice out on him."

It was.

"Hey, sweetie!" His voice came bouncing through the earpiece, good-natured and exuberant. "Want to come join me for some after-movie ice cream? I've got a seat at Bella's with your name on it."

"Sure, hon," she said. "Although I'll have to skip the ice cream. I just ingested my yearly fat intake in one sitting."

"With Joe?" Eric asked. "His mom made that many brownies?"

"No, actually—she wasn't here," Cassidy said. "It was just the two of us." She felt a dull pain shoot through her shoulder and realized Joe had just punched her lightly. Suddenly she remembered what he'd said about Eric's secret jealous streak. "But all we did was eat a ton of junk food and play Pictionary. And I really missed you—and I think you're hot."

"What?" Eric sounded confused but pleased.

"You heard me, hottie." Cassidy laughed. "See you in twenty."

"Did it work?" Joe asked eagerly.

"I have no idea," Cassidy said, hitting the End button on her cell phone. "He probably thought I was high or something."

"Well, you know, you *are* hanging out with a juvenile delinquent," Joe reminded her. "Camp Crackhead, here I come!"

Cassidy wrapped her arms around Joe once again and gave him a friendly hug. She couldn't help but think about how she was going to actually miss this skinny creature and his silly jokes, especially because the whole night had reminded her of how fun he was.

"Do me two favors this summer," she said. "First, don't get hooked on smack out there with all the junkies."

"I'll try not to," Joe said. "Don't . . . turn French or whatever. What's the other favor?"

"Send me some letters?"

"Will you be able to read my handwriting?" Joe laughed.

Cassidy kicked him on the legs, but gently. "Promise me you'll keep in touch, jerk, or else."

Joe took her hand in his and kissed it sweetly. "I promise."

Then Cassidy scampered down the ladder of the tree house and dashed off into the night in hopes that she'd enjoy her last few hours of summer freedom, even though she was worried that it wouldn't get much better than this.

Chapter Five

Monday, June 19

Cassidy darling,

Bonne chance on your first day of French class! We are so proud of you for getting into this program, and we know you'll be a huge success.

Don't forget to take good notes and block out two hours of quiet study time each night to maximize your productivity. Also, make sure there are whole grains in your breakfast and plenty of protein in your lunch to keep blood flowing to your brain all day long.

Here's a little present to keep you organized!

Love,
Mom

There was a packet of highlighters with color-coordinated Post-it tabs next to the note on the table. Cassidy left them where they were. She wasn't even supposed to start class until the next day, but as usual, her mother was thinking way in advance.

She grabbed her car keys off the hook labeled CASSIDY in the front hall and drove to Larissa's house.

"Hey, babe!" Larissa was already running out the front door. "Ready for some back-to-school shopping?"

Larissa slid into the passenger seat and plugged her iPod into the stereo system. The new Gwen Stefani song came blasting through the speakers.

"You mean back-to-*summer*-school," Cassidy corrected her.

"Whatever. Shopping's shopping."

In an unprecedented gesture of generosity, Larissa agreed to hit Cassidy's favorite stores first. But after a couple of hours at Theory, Banana Republic, and Kenneth Cole, Cassidy could tell Larissa was starting to get antsy.

"Can we *please* go somewhere where they've heard of colors other than khaki and black?" she begged, unwrapping a Twizzler outside Zara. "I'm going crazy here. You'd think we were shopping for preppy nuns or something."

"Fine," Cassidy agreed. She was already lugging around three huge bags, and the fluorescent lighting in the stores was starting to give her a headache. "Where do you want to go?"

"Well, actually," Larissa said, a naughty look in her eye, "they have some really cute stuff at Seersucker."

"Larissa," Cassidy said. "You know that stuff is too trendy for me."

"No way, dude. Some of it would look great on you! Like, there's this one skirt that I *think* is long enough for you to get away with wearing to school. And it's really *mostly* gray, except for these cute little green lizards. Come on, Cass, you'll totally love it."

"Fine," Cassidy agreed begrudgingly. "Although there's no way I'm wearing something that makes me look like I have reptiles crawling up my legs."

"It won't," Larissa assured her as they left the mall and headed toward the hip Malibu neighborhood where she'd be spending her summer days. She was already bounding out of the car as Cassidy struggled to parallel-park down the street.

"Larissa!" the girl at the counter cried when they entered Seersucker. She ran around the case holding faux-antique glass brooches and blew tiny air kisses on both Larissa's cheeks. She had to stand on her toes to do it. Fumiko was Japanese, with shaggy black hair swept to the side and long bangs. She wore a tank top with a *Knight Rider* logo on the front, a long skirt made from white gauze, denim, and netting, and a pair of those

Indian-style shoes with complicated gold embroidery on the pointed toes.

"Larissa's here?" There was a clacking sound and a wooden-beaded curtain parted to reveal Dina, the other owner of the store. She had long brown hair dreadlocked and pulled back in a messy ponytail and was wearing a vintage brown-and-white polka-dotted dress with cream-colored stiletto heels. There was a tattoo of the Wonder Woman insignia on her calf. "Hey, girl, how goes?"

"Great," Larissa said. "I can't wait to start working here. Oh, and I have some super ideas for the fashion show we're putting on this summer."

"Fab," Dina said.

"We'd love to hear them," Fumiko agreed.

As Larissa launched into a lengthy description of the faux fur they could use to line that season's blazers, Cassidy stood staring at her best friend in disbelief. Fumiko and Dina were acting like she wasn't even in the store, and Larissa hadn't bothered to introduce her. It was true that Larissa could be out of it at times, but it was unlike her to be downright rude.

Cassidy stood so that her shoulder was nearly touching Larissa's, hoping sheer physical proximity would be a big enough hint. But Larissa was so engrossed in her conversation that Cassidy could have blown in both her ears and she probably wouldn't have noticed. Cassidy felt her face go red with anger as the three of them chatted away about the fashion show. Had the blue-beaded necklace she'd just bought at Theory rendered her invisible or something? She was beginning to feel like an idiot—or even worse, a third wheel. Even though there were four of them in the store.

Well, if they were just going to ignore her, maybe she'd do some shopping after all. She wandered away from Larissa and toward the back of the store, occasionally checking out a price tag or stopping to roll a piece of fabric between her fingers. Normally if someone did that in a boutique, the staff would come running to see if you needed any help, but Fumiko and Dina just continued their endless conversation with her friend—the one that she, apparently, wasn't good enough to join.

She found the skirt with the lizards that Larissa had been talking about and picked it up, holding it against her body. The lizards were huge and bright green. No way would she ever wear something like that. What had Larissa been thinking? Didn't she know Cassidy's taste better?

After a while, Cassidy got bored with looking at clothes she would never wear and wandered over to where Larissa was leaning against the counter, still chattering away with her bosses about the fall line. If there was one thing Cassidy hated, it was interrupting people's conversations. The pacing seemed impossible—

waiting for a break and then hopping in with whatever you had to say, like playing double Dutch on the playground but a million times more nerve-racking. She stared at the brooches in the glass case. Some of them were actually kind of pretty, not that she was really the big-jewelry-wearing type.

"Can I help you with something?" Dina asked finally, clearly not recognizing her from when they had first walked into the store to ask for jobs.

"Oh, gosh, I'm sorry!" Larissa gasped. "I didn't even introduce you guys. Fumiko, Dina, this is Cassidy. She was supposed to work here with me this summer, but now she has to go to summer school instead."

"You must be crushed," Fumiko said stoically. "I bet you would have much rather worked here."

"Yeah, maybe," Cassidy said. Half an hour ago, she would have agreed wholeheartedly, but all of a sudden she wasn't so sure. Would she really want to work with people who made Larissa momentarily forget she existed? Or was she just overreacting because she was upset about summer school?

"We're sorry we can't get you too, but at least we have Larissa," Dina said. "She has so much energy and such cool ideas. We're both psyched she's working here."

Cassidy decided she was definitely overreacting as Larissa beamed at the compliment, her eyes glowing like the brooches in the case below her. Cassidy tried to suppress the surge of envy and unhappiness that shot through her stomach.

"You should be," she said, hoping none of the heaviness in her heart had crept into her voice. "Larissa's a lot of fun."

*   *   *

Cassidy pulled her mom's old Volvo into the student parking lot in front of the Seaver Academics complex at the Pepperdine campus and took a deep breath. The bright California sun was ricocheting off her Kenneth Cole shades and giving her a slight headache. Then again, perhaps the throbbing in her temples was due to stress and not the strength of UV rays.

Here goes, she thought. *The beginning of the end.* She grabbed the black DKNY book bag she'd filled that morning with a notebook, pens and, of course, her sketchbook and sighed deeply as she tried to prepare herself for the first day of what she'd already begun to think of as the Worst Summer Since 'N Sync Broke Up.

Her fears were confirmed the moment she walked in the door. The room was half full of students who looked like they just couldn't *wait* to crack their *Français Maintenant* textbooks. A girl up front in a neatly pressed polo shirt and khakis smiled perkily at Cassidy as she brushed past to find a seat near the back, over by the window, where she could stare out at the lush green lawn and long for four thirty to come.

When she sat down, a husky guy with black hair spiked up in the middle of his head like a Kewpie doll and thick, round glasses entered, looked around, and made a beeline for the seat next to hers.

"Hi there," he said, sitting down with a grunt. He extended his hand. It was large and slightly sweaty when she shook it. "I'm Benjy. Benjy Kahn. Or, I guess, *je m'appelle* Benjy Kahn or whatever, since this is French and all."

"I'm Cassidy," she replied. No way she was going to start blathering away in a foreign language until she was forced to.

"Guess you're not into the whole 'speaking French unprovoked' thing, are you?" Benjy said, making air quotes with his fingers.

"Not really."

"Me either." He shrugged. "So are you trying to beef up your transcript or something? Because just between you and me, I think ninety percent of our fellow students are only in this for the extra credit."

"Are you?" Cassidy asked.

Benjy laughed. "I guess you could say that. Either that, or I'm seriously into taking French in the summertime, volunteering with the fire department, bringing cookies to the elderly, learning astronomy on Thursday nights, and managing the varsity fencing team. But when Harvard gets my application, guess who's gonna look well rounded?"

"Harvard, huh?" Cassidy pulled out her notebook and a pen, glancing at the color-coded Post-it notes and thinking how Benjy and her mom would be BFFs. If they ever met, she would spend the rest of her life having to hear about how *integrated* and *achievement-oriented* he was.

"Only school worth going to," Benjy said. Cassidy ignored him and was in the middle of turning off the ringer on her cell when the door banged open and a woman in her fifties with wispy hair, a slightly out-of-style business suit, and a small run in her stockings rushed into the room.

"Ah, *bonjour, bonjour!*" she said, slightly out of breath. *"Je m'appelle Madame Briand. Bienvenue à la course française!"*

"Bonjour!" the girl up front in the polo shirt chirped. Madame Briand's head jerked up and her eyes registered a startled look before she broke into a huge smile. Benjy glanced at Cassidy and rolled his eyes.

Madame Briand set a leather satchel on her chair, removed a large stack of photocopied papers, and set them down on her desk with a smack.

"I'm so happy that you've all decided to enroll in this course," she continued in an accent that Cassidy couldn't quite place. It wasn't French, but it was close. "This will be a summer of learning and exploration, of hard study, intensive research and, dare I say, a bit of fun."

Fun didn't sound so bad, but the rest of it Cassidy could do without.

"You see," Madame Briand continued, "I've developed a unique method for the study of language, and I am pleased to be passing it along to you. I believe that one does not learn a language merely by reading a textbook. *Non!*" She picked up the *Français Maintenant* textbook and flung it on the floor. The entire class gasped.

"There is more to the beautiful French language than what you find in a book," Madame Briand continued. "It is a language of intrigue, mystery, and romance. After all, it is a Romance language. And so we will learn French by *speaking* French and by *experiencing* French culture with our eyes and ears, our lips and tongues, our hearts and souls."

She pressed her hand to her chest and took a deep breath before plunging back into a torrent of speech. Cassidy couldn't believe a woman as frumpy-looking as Madame Briand could talk so much and so quickly. "We'll be visiting institutions where the French language and culture are still alive and well, conversing with one another in French, drinking in the French atmosphere like a fine glass of Pernod."

Well, that sounded good at least. Cassidy didn't

know what Pernod was, but it sounded delicious and highly alcoholic.

"However," Madame Briand added, "one must also study the intricacies of the language, the grammar and vocabulary, usage and syntax." She stooped to pick the textbook off the floor, blew the dust from its cover, then wiped it across the front of her skirt for good measure, smiling sheepishly at her antics. "And so we will be using the textbook after all. Sorry to disappoint you."

Cassidy immediately slumped in her chair and began thinking of what Eric was doing at this very moment. Probably running around on the sand in his tropical-print board shorts or greasing up his supple skin with some coconut-smelling lotion. She thought about how great he looked with his shirt off and how excellent it felt every time she pressed up against him. Then her mouth began to water.

Being here is worse than getting two Brazilian waxes in a row, she thought. (Not that she knew what getting even one felt like—she'd just heard from Larissa that it was very painful.)

"And now we will take a look at the curriculum," Madame Briand continued. She began passing out the photocopied pages. "As you can see, the focus will be on conversation and experiential education, but you will also have weekly quizzes on vocabulary and grammar.

These will be on Mondays, so you'll have the weekend to study."

Didn't she mean the weekend to *worry*? Cassidy always spent the day before a test in a cold sweat. As if going to class all week wasn't bad enough, now she had to spend her weekends cramming too?

Make that three Brazilian waxes.

"And at the end of the eight weeks, you will have a final exam," Madame Briand said. "This will be a ten-minute oral presentation in which you speak in front of the class about a French cultural subject of your choice."

Cassidy felt the blood freeze in her veins. *An oral presentation in front of the whole class?* That was like her worst nightmare! She couldn't even have a ten-second conversation with the mailman without stuttering, let alone blab away for ten whole minutes in front of thirty people.

"*À maintenant,*" Madame Briand said. "A bit about me. You see, I am from Montréal" (she pronounced it *Mohn-ray-ahl*), "where French is an official, government-sanctioned language." She smiled and pressed her hand to her heart, as if there were a tiny piece of *Mohn-ray-ahl* still lodged there.

The girl in the polo shirt raised her hand.

"*Oui?*" Madame Briand called on her.

"Have you ever been to the Montréal Independent Film Festival?" she asked, her voice laced with smugness.

"Actually, no, I have not," Madame Briand replied.

"Oh, you should go! I went last year and it was fabulous. You Canadians have so much talent!"

"Why, um . . . *merci*?" Madame Briand seemed to be deciding to take this as a compliment.

Cassidy couldn't believe it. If this program was so damn prestigious, why couldn't they find a French teacher who was actually French?

"And now let us all get to know each other," Madame Briand continued. "We will go around the room and introduce ourselves—*en français, bien sûr*—and tell the class a little something about ourselves. Also in French, naturally."

Cassidy cringed as the students began introducing themselves. Most of them said simple things, like that they liked to ski or they had a brother named Phil. But the girl who thought Canadians had talent introduced herself as Cecilia, and went on to say that she had traveled the world with her parents, was also taking Italian and Japanese, and wanted to go into international politics. Cassidy found herself wishing Cecilia would hurry up and go *somewhere* international and never come back.

As it got closer to her turn to speak, Cassidy's hands began to get clammy. Just the thought of talking in front of everyone made her want to puke. She wondered what would happen if she suddenly opened the window and jumped out. But that would not only draw attention to her, but probably would also get her a broken leg, so she'd be stuck in French class *and* hobbling around on crutches for the rest of the summer. What could be worse?

Then the door to the classroom opened and Cassidy forgot everything, including her own name. The guy who walked in was a dead ringer for Chad Michael Murray, but not quite as tall, and with crazy brown hair that seemed to defy gravity and spike up in all directions like he'd stuck his finger in an electrical outlet. He entered the room with the kind of easy confidence basketball players display running up and down the court, and the corners of his lips curled up in an impish smile as he surveyed the class.

He wore paint-spattered jeans and a short-sleeved black button-down shirt. Cassidy could just see the edge of a tattoo on the tight brown bicep peeking out from under the edge of his sleeve and wondered dizzily what it was. But the most arresting thing about him was his eyes. They were the color of the Pacific Ocean first thing in the morning, a deep, mysterious green with miles of meaning underneath.

He said something quickly to the teacher in French— the only words Cassidy could catch were "sorry," "late," and "wrong room." Was this guy actually going to be in her class?

Madame Briand turned to the group and beamed.

"Crickets," she said. *Crickets?* "I'd like to introduce Zach Weston. He'll be your TA this summer, and I'm sure he'll be an enormous help in the classroom. Zach is a student at NYU, but he spent last summer studying abroad in Paris."

Benjy was rolling his eyes at Cassidy again, but she barely noticed. She was too busy taking in the way Zach's chin angled into a point and the amazing magnetism that seemed to electrify the air around him.

"Hi, everyone," Zach said, smiling. Was it just her imagination or was he looking straight at her? "Glad to be here."

Madame Briand looked at Zach like she wanted to adopt him before instructing the group to resume introductions. Cassidy stared at the back of Zach's neck as he took a seat in the front of the classroom, at the tiny golden hairs skimming his smooth brown skin. Her palms were moist and clammy, and not just because she was nervous about talking to the class. She hadn't felt this kind of instant attraction to someone since she first saw Eric ride a fifteen-foot wave at Point Dume. In fact, even though she'd been thinking of Eric a few moments before, she could barely picture him now. Everything was just so . . . foggy.

"*Et tu?*" Madame Briand was saying. And then, louder: "*Comment t'appelles-tu?*"

Cassidy looked up to realize the whole class was staring at her. Great. She'd been so into drooling over Zach, she'd practically forgotten where she was.

"*Je m'appelle* C-Cassidy Jones," she stammered, realizing she hadn't thought of anything to say after that. She dug frantically in her head, trying to remember a single one of the French phrases she'd learned in school. But maddeningly, she could only come up with *voulez-vous couchez avec moi ce soir*. Asking Zach to sleep with her that night wouldn't be the most appropriate thing to say.

"*Bonjour,* Cassidy!"

Cassidy looked up just in time to catch the end of her name coming from Zach's lips. This time, he was looking right at her, and he was definitely smiling. The warmest, most dazzling smile she'd ever seen.

Chapter Six

Dear Cassidy,

Hey, how's it going?

So I made it out to Idaho in one piece, but I can't
promise you I'll come back in one. Our "base camp"
is at the top of a mountain that the bus could barely
drive up because the road is so steep and winding, I
guess because they don't want us to escape or something. Not that I know where I'd escape to, since the
nearest town is fifty miles away. Our lodgings kind
of resemble a federal prison. We're in this concrete
dorm with creaky bunk beds, and at first I was
pleased to see I'd gotten a bottom bunk—until I met
Lloyd, the guy above me, who weighs three hundred

pounds and says he was busted for "dust," whatever
that is. He tosses and turns all night, and every time
he rolls over it sounds like a five-car collision, so if
I'm not making much sense, it may be because I'm
sleep-deprived.

We had our first "group" this morning. They're
all into doing things outdoors (*even going to the
bathroom—that's what the creepy outhouses are for. I
guess indoor plumbing is too much to ask for*), so we
had to sit around in a circle in this grove of pine
trees. In case you were wondering, shorts and pine
needles do NOT mix. Anyway, I'm a little freaked out
by the other kids here. We all had to say what we're here
for and, suffice to say, I was embarrassed to admit I'm
here for pot that I don't even smoke. Everyone else was
doing like twelve tabs of Ecstasy every night or smoking
crack. You know how when we say, "Are you smoking
crack?" we're usually joking? Yeah. Not these kids.
Some of them have actually smoked crack. A lot of it.
Which doesn't exactly make you a pleasant person to be
around, as it turns out.

Lloyd wanted to know if I'd smuggled anything in,
which would be hard, considering they had dogs sniff-
ing our bags when we got here. Even my Cadburys
were confiscated!

Anyway, I have to go. I have "KP," which means
slopping gruel into everyone's plastic bowls for dinner.

Our silverware is plastic too, I guess so we don't kill each other with it.

The secret of this boy is that he wants to go home. I hope your summer is better than mine so far, but I don't see how it couldn't be.

Cheers,
Joe

Cassidy had to admit that her summer was going a *little* better than Joe's was, even though they were barely at the end of June. It turned out that Madame Briand's "cultural immersion" policy included a lot of field trips, and Cassidy was actually kind of psyched that the first was to the J. Paul Getty Museum, featuring an exhibit of French impressionist art on loan from the Metropolitan Museum of Art in New York City. As she followed the teacher's voice through the cool, echoing marble halls, she wondered why she didn't go to museums more often. She couldn't decide which she loved more: losing herself in the deep, richly colored paintings or being able to just stand there and think her own thoughts without having to talk.

"And here is a Degas." Madame Briand pointed to a picture of a girl in a pink tutu. "He was obsessed with the French ballet, but most of all with the children. They were called *les petits rats*—the little rats."

"That's what I call my kid brothers," Benjy whispered in Cassidy's ear. "And they don't wear tutus, either."

Cassidy rolled her eyes. Ever since they'd gotten to the museum, Benjy had attached himself to her side as if he were assigned to be her own personal not-very-funny stand-up comic for the duration of the trip. Every time he leaned in to subject her to another lame attempt at wit, the cheesy smell from the Brie he'd eaten on the way over wafted into her nostrils. Not that she was trying to hang on Madame Briand's every word or anything, but she kind of wished he would just shut up and let her enjoy the exhibit.

Cassidy glanced over at the most beautiful piece of artwork in the room—Zach. He was standing a bit away from the rest of the group with his thumbs tucked casually into his belt loops, smiling his usual bemused smile. In the week since she'd first seen him, Cassidy couldn't figure out what his exact purpose in the classroom was. Occasionally he joined the conversation, his deep, soft voice sending shivers up Cassidy's spine. But he didn't talk nearly as much as, say, Cecilia, who Cassidy was more than ready to ship *par avion* as far away from Malibu as humanly possible. Every once in a while Zach led a discussion, but mostly he just sat up front, angled half toward the class and half toward the teacher, quietly driving Cassidy crazy with his undeniable sexiness.

Sometimes she thought he was looking at her too. But only sometimes.

She watched as his eyes slid toward her, locking with hers. *Ugh, he caught me staring again.* Her face burst into flames as she looked frantically around the room for something to focus on that didn't turn her insides into sweet, mushy Quaker maple brown sugar oatmeal. *The guy probably thinks I'm* Looney Tunes, she thought miserably.

Her eyes landed on a painting that covered almost an entire wall, and showed people in Victorian garb enjoying a sunny day in the park. From where Cassidy stood, the people appeared blurry around the edges, but as she walked toward the painting to take a closer look, the image separated into thousands of tiny dots, like the pixels in an image online that hadn't fully loaded. There were hundreds of shades, none of them blended, and Cassidy found it fascinating.

She didn't know how long she'd been lost in the painting when someone came up behind her. Why couldn't Benjy just go away? She stared stubbornly ahead of her, noticing the subtlety of the colors even as she tried to will him out of her personal space.

"C'est belle, non?" he finally said.

Benjy speaking French when he didn't have to—now *that* was a first!

Except that it wasn't Benjy. It was the low, raspy voice she spent all day, every day aching to hear. Zach.

Suddenly Cassidy was afraid to turn around. Afraid that if she did, Zach would see the deep red flush spreading across her cheeks and realize the effect he had on her.

"Um, yeah," she murmured, still facing the painting. "It's really nice."

Nice?!? That was what you said about a Hallmark card, not great art. But it was hard to come up with anything better with Zach so close she could feel his breath on her neck as he spoke. No wonder she was turning into a bigger space cadet than Trishelle from *The Real World: Las Vegas.* She hoped he couldn't see her shivering.

"It's a style called pointillism," he said. "Tiny brushstrokes all coming together to form a whole. It doesn't make any sense from up close, but when you get farther away, the picture comes out. Seurat pioneered it."

"I wish I could do that," Cassidy said quietly.

"Yeah? Are you an artist too?"

Only if drawing dumb little cartoons counts as art, Cassidy thought.

"No, not really. I just like to draw sometimes."

"You know, from the way you're standing," said Zach, his voice so low he was nearly whispering, "I can't tell if you're talking to me or the painting."

Cassidy laughed out loud before she could catch herself. "Well," she countered, "you're standing so close that if I turn around now, I'll be stepping on your toes."

"This better?" Zach took a step back and Cassidy found herself facing him. From that close it was impossible to concentrate on anything but the fascinating symmetry of his face. Who knew people could be that hot? Cassidy felt her confidence draining away again. She was back to square one, staring like an idiot. How could she possibly have a crush like this when her heart belonged to someone else? That just didn't make any sense to her.

"I noticed you were checking out that painting for a while," Zach continued. "It's not every day you see someone who really appreciates art. It really got on my nerves when I was living in Paris. All these idiotic American tourists who only went to the Louvre to snap a picture of the *Mona Lisa*. It's like they were looking at art without even really seeing it."

"No offense," Cassidy said, finally finding her tongue, "but weren't you kind of an idiotic tourist? I mean, you are American and all."

Instead of being offended, Zach threw back his head and laughed.

"It's true," he said. "You totally called me on it. What are you going to accuse me of next?"

"I don't know," Cassidy mused. "Maybe standing here talking to me when the rest of the class you're supposedly TA'ing has moved on to the next room?"

"Hey, I know a worthy student when I see one," Zach said. "I mean, haven't you already benefited from my expertise?"

"I guess I have," Cassidy said. "But what about the

rest of the class? You're depriving them of your genius as we speak."

"So what are you going to do?" Zach wiggled his eyebrows, making her smile. "Report me?"

"That depends," Cassidy countered. "Are you going to do anything I'd need to report?"

Holy crap, was she actually *flirting*? She had never flirted before in her life. That required being outgoing and courageous, neither of which Cassidy ever felt like she was. *Larissa* flirted. Cassidy just quietly observed.

What had gotten into her? And what would Eric do if he knew? He was all wary before when she was hanging out with an old friend like Joe. One look at the way she was salivating over Zach and he'd probably hire a private investigator to follow her around and make sure she wasn't doing anything sinful.

"I'll be an absolute angel, I promise," Zach assured her, and she felt a small surge of disappointment.

"Tell me about the rest of this exhibit." She reminded herself once again that she had a boyfriend. This would just be for educational purposes, she decided. "Madame Briand's been going on and on about how *French* everything is, but you seem to know a lot more about the art itself."

"I'm hardly an expert." Zach's smile seemed to stir the gooey oatmeal her insides had become. "But I can maybe tell you a few things."

Cassidy was relieved to let Zach play tour guide, and he seemed happy to finally get to spout some of the knowledge he'd picked up trolling the museums in Paris. Cassidy only hoped he wouldn't catch on that she was staring at him more than at the paintings. As they talked, he led her through a glassed-in atrium and out a side door to a wide green lawn filled with large, modern steel sculptures.

"Where are we?" she asked. "Won't Madame Briand notice we're missing?"

"Believe me," Zach assured her, "Madame Briand wouldn't notice if her head was missing from her shoulders. Don't get me wrong, she's a good teacher, but man, is she flaky!"

"She is?" Cassidy hadn't noticed. Maybe because she spent all her time in class imagining Zach with his strong, perfectly toned arms around her.

"Why do you think they have me there? I help her keep all the students' names straight, and after she grades your papers, she gives them to me to hand back. It's because she can't keep track of who's who. Half the time she calls Cecilia by your name."

"No!" Cassidy gasped in mock horror.

"Yes!" Zach rolled his eyes. "It hurts me too."

"Well, I'm not surprised, really," Cassidy said. She imitated Cecilia's high-pitched whine. "Because my parents have taken me to independent film festivals all over the world and I want to live in twelve countries simultaneously when I grow up, which should be like five minutes from now because I'm so mo-ti-vated."

Zach's easy laugh rang out over the garden as he sat down on an intricately carved wooden bench under a willow tree and patted the empty seat next to him. Cassidy hesitated a moment, then joined him. If she were an inch closer, their thighs would be touching. Not that she noticed or anything.

"So why did you decide to spend your summer doing this?" Cassidy was genuinely curious . . . about everything there was to know about him.

"Because I can." Zach shrugged. "I needed something to do, and this gives me college credit and a place to live. It sure beats going home."

"Home?" Cassidy asked.

"Oklahoma." Zach winced. "Not exactly an intellectual hotbed. I was happy to get out."

"I guess France was about as far away as you could get."

"Exactly." Zach laughed. "Man, Oklahoma was completely not my scene."

"So what's your scene?" Cassidy asked. "Paris?"

"Anything new," Zach said. "I loved Paris because when I first got there, I wasn't fluent in French, so I had to learn to read people based on their faces instead of what they said. It taught me a lot."

"That must have been so weird," Cassidy mused. "Living in a foreign country where you don't even speak the language."

"It was great." Zach's eyes glittered. "I'd just spend hours wandering the streets, getting totally lost and suddenly coming out on something so beautiful, like a park or a building or a sculpture garden."

"That must have been incredible." Cassidy sighed. "I wish I could get lost sometimes, but I've lived here my whole life. I could drive through Malibu with my eyes closed and not get in an accident."

"I wouldn't try that if I were you," Zach said, putting his hand mindlessly on her bare knee for a split second. Cassidy nearly jumped, but he didn't seem to catch on to the fact that he stimulated every fiber of her being by mere skin-to-skin contact. "Being here kind of reminds me of high school, actually. Although it wasn't a great experience for me. I'd hang out with the same two people all the time because I was too shy to talk to anyone else."

"*You* were too shy?" Cassidy asked incredulously.

"Oh yeah. I just couldn't get my mind around having an actual conversation with anyone but Ted and Jimmy. I *wanted* to, but there was just no way. Every time I tried, my mouth went all dry and I'd start to shake." Cassidy herself was shaking a bit. Her leg was bouncing up and down nervously as Zach's deep, intense gaze kept shining on her.

"But . . . you're a TA now," she managed to say. "That means you talk to people all the time, right? You even get up in front of the class and *teach*. There's no way I could ever do something like that."

"You'd be surprised. Going to Paris changed everything. I was all alone, I didn't have Ted and Jimmy to fall back on anymore. It was either learn how to talk to strangers or let my vocal cords atrophy from neglect. I mean, if I hadn't spoken to anyone all last summer, nobody would have *cared*. I think that's what finally got me over it, not having anyone try to bring me out of my shell. I just had to do it on my own."

Cassidy was really floored by this admission. Zach was so open and seemed like he had no secrets at all. He was just laying his whole life out on the table, and all of it was so fascinating. Cassidy wished that she could learn how to do the same, but the funny thing was, suddenly she was hopeful that she'd be able to learn. Zach's anecdote helped her to see that changing was not only possible, it was inevitable.

"So, hey," Zach said. "I'm sure you're totally fed up with all this 'experience French culture' crap, but on the off chance you're not, do you want to catch a Godard film at the revival house this Friday? He's like the quintessential French new-wave director, if you're into that kind of stuff."

"Will I be quizzed afterward?" Cassidy joked. She

couldn't believe she had even gotten the words out. Inside, her head was spinning faster than a Tilt-A-Whirl. Was Zach asking her out?

"Yes," Zach said. "But I'll let you cheat."

Cheat. The word echoed in her ears, making her think suddenly of Eric. Would going to the movies with Zach be cheating? Her eyes fluttered around the garden as she tried to think of an answer that Larissa might say. Most likely something gross like, "If there's no penetration, then it doesn't really count," but who knew these days— Larissa had been pretty MIA of late, just like Eric. Then Cassidy's gaze darted down to her watch. It took a moment for the position of the hands to register, and when it did, she let out a small gasp. She was supposed to meet Eric at the beach thirty-five minutes ago.

"I have to get going," she said abruptly. "I'm totally late to meet my friend." Her *friend*? Since when did she refer to Eric as her *friend*?

Zach shrugged, and Cassidy thought she saw a hint of disappointment flicker in his eyes. "Have fun," he said as she reluctantly stood up to leave. She turned and began walking away from him across the lawn.

"Hey," he called after her. She stopped mid-step and turned to look at him. He seemed to glow in the late-afternoon sunlight, his body relaxed and fluid against the bench.

"How about that movie?" he yelled.

"Okay!" she said, the jolt of adrenaline that shot through her propelling her the rest of the way to her car.

Her heart was still pounding when she slid into the driver's seat of the Volvo and turned on her cell. She'd missed two texts and a voice message from Eric, wondering where she was.

Class ran L8–C U soon, she texted back before turning on the engine and steering the old Volvo down to the beach. *Why did I say yes to Zach?* she wondered as she cranked open the window, letting the breeze cool her still-burning cheeks. For that matter, why had she told Zach she was late to meet a *friend*? She always referred to Eric as her boyfriend; normally, it was something she felt really proud of.

Well, she rationalized, *it's not like it's a date or anything.* For all she knew, they'd be going in a big group. Then it *definitely* wouldn't be a date, right? She found herself hoping that Zach had asked half the class to go as well. Except she realized that she really hoped he hadn't.

Chapter Seven

Eric and two of his surfing buddies were throwing a Frisbee down the shoreline of Zuma Beach to a big, happy golden retriever when Cassidy arrived. The dog ran up to her, drooling around the Frisbee's plastic rim as he deposited it at her feet. Cassidy picked it up gingerly, trying not to touch any slobber, before tossing it to Eric. She shaded her eyes against the sun's glare as she watched the Frisbee arc into the sky over the ocean. The dog went tearing after it, the pale fur on his hind legs fluttering in the wind. He nearly collided with Eric, and the two of them fell to the sand, wrestling playfully as each tried to get ahold of the Frisbee. Cassidy could hear the affection in Eric's voice as he spoke to the dog, and she felt a surge of tenderness rush to her heart. Eric was a really good guy. She'd loved him for two years, and nothing could change that.

"Hi, sweetheart!" Eric trotted up to her and wrapped her in a bear hug. "I was worried about you. Why'd you have to stay so late after class today?"

Cassidy ran her hands over his chiseled chest. "We were at the Getty Museum."

"Yikes," he said, wincing. "Were you totally bored?"

"Actually, no. There was this French impressionist exhibit and they had a painting by this guy Seurat who used tiny dots to create this big beautiful picture. It's called pointillism. It was amazing."

Eric looked puzzled but kept a crooked grin on his face. "Sounds cool."

Cassidy felt vaguely annoyed. That Seurat painting had burrowed itself into her heart, and all Eric could say was that it sounded "cool"? But that was just Eric. Art wasn't really his thing. Eric liked things you could surf on or throw a Frisbee to. He wasn't stupid or anything, just a physical kind of guy. Even so, she kind of wished he could appreciate the transformative power the experience had had over her. She'd even considered taking her art skills to the next level by sketching some nature scenes or drawing the bowl of fruit that sat on her mother's precious Domain dining table. Eric had never taken an interest in this passion of hers, and for the first time Cassidy was wondering how much that would affect their future together.

Eric kissed her cheek gently and pulled her out of her thoughts. "So Tim's having a luau farther down the beach—kind of as a pre–July Fourth party. You up for some roasted pig and hula dancing?"

"Roasted pig?" Cassidy said. "You have *got* to be kidding."

"I'm not," Eric said. "Come on, I'll show you."

He grabbed her hand and began pulling her along the thick, warm sand as she giggled into the wind. As they got closer to the party sounds coming from near the pier, Eric slowed down and began nervously swinging her hand in his.

"I really missed you at the movies the other night," he murmured.

"I missed you too," Cassidy said. "But it was good that I could give Joe some moral support. I mean, he was getting shipped off for the whole summer, and he needed someone to talk to."

"Yeah?" asked Eric. She could tell he was struggling to keep his voice casual. "So what did you guys talk about, anyway?"

"Oh, you know," Cassidy said vaguely. She didn't want to admit that she'd confided in Joe about their relationship. She knew that would only feed Eric's insecurities. "Just, like, how we were both going to have crappy summers."

"You didn't do anything besides talk, did you?" Eric looked off at the waves, not meeting her eyes.

Cassidy squeezed his hand. "Of course not. He's just a friend."

He finally turned to face her, the wrinkles in his forehead relaxing into relief, but he still seemed uneasy. She thought back to what Joe had said in the tree house. She knew she had to say something reassuring, something that would make Eric feel like he was the only guy for her. She searched her heart for the right words, but it was difficult to find them. And she knew why. This crush on Zach had shaken her up more than she'd thought. There was a variety of things she could profess to Eric, but she suddenly doubted her sincerity so much it made her feel sick to her stomach. Luckily, she managed to squeak out something nice.

"I'd never want to be without you," she said. It was actually very true—she couldn't picture her life without him in it somehow.

She watched Eric's face break into a big smile before he reached down and gathered her in his arms. He picked her up and swung her around as she laughed and kicked her legs in the air.

"So I'm your one and only?" He set her down, tenderly brushing her hair back from her face.

"Absolutely," she said confidently, even though Zach's face flashed through her mind. This was so unsettling. Here she was with her handsome, sweet, thoughtful, kind boyfriend and she couldn't get her TA out of her head.

It's not like Zach would even give her the time of day. They'd had *one* conversation, and he'd asked her to go see a foreign film, which meant nothing in the grand scheme of college guy hookups. But it didn't even matter. Cassidy was in her boyfriend's arms and it didn't feel the same as it did a few weeks ago.

*   *   *

Cassidy and Eric spent the next four hours settling in at the pier. The sunset had been beautiful—the pink and purple hues in the sky blended together beautifully—and now twilight was upon them. Eric's friends had marked an area of sand with tiki torches and dug a deep fire pit, filling it with coals and erecting a makeshift spit above. A whole pig turned slowly on the spit, the fat dripping off and into the crackling fire below. A bright red apple glowed in its open mouth.

The sound of Don Ho's music blared from the open trunk of a Lexus RX, and a few tipsy girls were trying to spin hula hoops on their gyrating hips. Cassidy saw their faces, flushed and laughing, in the glow of the fire.

"Hungry?" Eric asked her. "That pig looks great!"

Cassidy didn't feel too fabulous about eating a creature when she could still look it in the eyes. Instead she took a bottle of Heineken out of a blue plastic cooler and sipped it as Eric ran off to join an impromptu game of coconut volleyball. Obviously he was relieved after their little talk. She found a dry patch of beach away from the fire to sit on before removing the white strappy kitten-heeled Marc Jacobs sandals she'd worn to class and wiggled her toes in the cool sand.

Taking a long swallow of beer, she tilted her head back to stare up at the stars. It was so clear out she could see the Milky Way. She'd learned in science class that it was actually millions of stars that were quite far apart, but because of the way the galaxy curved, people saw it as a stripe across the sky. Like the Seurat: millions of tiny dots that made a picture when you looked at them the right way. Thinking of the painting made her day-dream of Zach, which made her run her hands up and down her goose-bumpy arms, feeling the silky hairs stand up against her palm.

"Hey, babe." Eric stood above her, stretching out his hands and pulling her to her feet. "I brought you something."

He settled a garland of brightly colored cloth flowers around her neck, gently lifting her hair up over it. "You looked like you needed to get lei'd."

Cassidy laughed as he wrapped his arms around her waist and drew her toward him. "You are so beautiful," he murmured. "I'm so lucky to have you, Cassidy. I can't wait until our anniversary. I have a special surprise in the works."

The last time she'd heard the word *surprise*, it turned out to be summer school. But looking up into Eric's eager brown eyes, she knew it would be something good. Maybe even an "I love you." And if it was, would she be ready—and willing—to say those words back to him? If someone had asked Cassidy that a month ago, she would have said yes. As the image of Zach's sexy grin floated through her brain for the eighty-eighth time that week (not that she was counting or anything), Cassidy realized that she wasn't one hundred percent sure of much of anything anymore.

Eric's kiss was warm and sweet. Cassidy felt herself melt—it was that good. All her thoughts from earlier that day (the stars and the Milky Way, the Seurat and Zach and the movie they were supposed to see together, Zach's breath on her neck) ran out through her loose, buzzing limbs and down the beach, disappearing into the dark, gentle waves lapping at the sand.

All except one.

I wonder if kissing Zach would feel better than this.

Chapter Eight

Ma chère Cassidy,

Your parents tell me you are studying French this summer. How wonderful! So you will be fluent when you come to stay with me in college, non? I hope you will consider it. I have a lovely house by the sea in Nice, and there is a guest room overlooking the beach. There is also a very nice young man next door who I would like you to meet. His name is François, and he is studying to be a doctor. You could do worse. . . .

Love,
Aunt Geraldine

Cassidy stared into the mirror and frowned. In her black silk ABS blouse and knee-length Calvin Klein skirt, she looked like she was going to the opera or a funeral, not out to a movie with a friend. She sighed, unzipped the skirt, and tossed it onto the growing pile of rejected clothes on her bed.

Why was it so hard to figure out what to wear? Oh, right. Larissa wasn't around to advise her on the creation of the perfect "I'm going on a kinda, sorta date with my kinda, sorta teacher" ensemble. She'd texted Larissa three times already; the most recent one was actually just the number 911. Larissa was kind enough to write back: U R NOT DYING. IT MUST WAIT. SS MADNESS! Apparently Cassidy would have to face the music without her. This wasn't cool at all.

As she dug her way to the back of her closet, Cassidy's eyes lit on the tight spaghetti-strap tank top Larissa had insisted she buy the last time they hit Bebe. It was cut just low enough to reveal a tiny bit of cleavage, and if she wore it with low-slung denim capris, it would show off a sliver of her stomach too. She added her favorite woven straw wedges from Nine West and turned sideways to look in the mirror.

She had to admit, she looked pretty hot. Kind of a sassy 1950s look, like Audrey Hepburn but crossed with some twenty-first-century attitude.

Not that it matters, she admonished herself even as she

reached for her L'Oreal Double Extend mascara, which Larissa always said made her lashes so long she could trip over them. *This is* not *a date. You're just going on an educational outing with your TA.*

Regardless, Cassidy could feel the mascara wand shivering slightly in her hand. She had told Eric that she had to spend the evening boning up for a French exam. She felt pretty bad lying, even though it was really only half a lie. She *was* going to see a French film, which could sort of be construed as preparing for a test. Cassidy stared at herself full on in the mirror. She got closer so that she could examine her face. And when she did, she could hear Joe's voice in her head.

You're the kind of girl who could never tell a lie.

Thankfully, her parents were at a book publicity function—the last thing she wanted to do was lie to them about who she was spending her evening with.

*　　*　　*

"You look great!" Zach said, kissing her lightly on both cheeks outside the vintage-looking Aero Theatre in Santa Monica. Cassidy mindlessly touched the spot on her right cheek where Zach had kissed her, which was practically on the corner of her lips. Then she realized that this was something a schoolgirl would do if she lusted after her teacher, so she pretended to brush a strand of hair out of her face. By the way Zach was still eyeing her, she doubted that he was fooled.

Speaking of eyefuls, Cassidy thought as she noticed how great Zach looked too. He'd swapped his usual black button-down shirt for a formfitting plain white T-shirt that hugged every curve on his chest and shoulders. There was no doubt about this—the guy worked out and *damn*, did it show. The other thing that showed was his tattoo—the sleeves were only covering a small portion of it, and now Cassidy's gaze became fixated on the hottest-looking arm she'd ever seen in her life.

"What is this?" she asked, pointing to his bicep. "I've been curious about it since day one."

Zach obligingly pushed up his sleeve, revealing an abstract design of interlocked squares and circles.

"It's nothing, really," he said. "My friend Pierre designed it. He's a student at the Paris Academy of Art. I got drunk one night and said I wanted him to make me a tattoo, and then when I sobered up, I felt bad telling him I changed my mind, so I just went ahead and got it."

Cassidy laughed as he ushered her into the cool, red-velvet lobby of the revival house. "Don't you feel weird having something on your skin forever that you didn't even choose?" she asked.

"Nah," he said. "It's like fate, you know? It's just a part of me."

"That's crazy," Cassidy said, impressed. Nobody she knew would do something like that. Eric was a take-things-as-they-come kind of guy, but he didn't have that kind of wild streak, the kind where he'd let someone else decide what was going to go on his skin forever.

"Do you really think it's crazy?" Zach asked, escorting her toward the popcorn stand.

"Not *bad* crazy," Cassidy assured him. "Just crazy like—that's not something anyone I know would do. I think it's cool, though."

"Thanks." Zach beamed. He insisted on buying them popcorn (and slathering it in gooey butter), but Cassidy's stomach was so jumpy from being within fifty yards of him that she was sure she wouldn't be able to eat.

"You're going to love this film," Zach said confidently. Cassidy just loved how that self-assuredness oozed out of him whenever he spoke or stood silently. In fact, she figured that it probably oozed out even when he slept. "It's very strange, but beautiful. If you're an artist, you'll definitely be into it."

Just as the lights began to dim, she caught Zach throwing her a thin, glimmering smile. She was so antsy, she could feel her knee bobbing up and down uncontrollably. Then she began crossing her legs and uncrossing them, which lasted all the way through the previews. Zach was so calm and secure, though. He was just grinning knowingly and munching on his popcorn, as if he anticipated that something wonderful was about to happen.

Once Cassidy tapped into Zach's vibe—an hour later—she was finally relaxed enough to pay attention to the movie, which was called *Une femme est une femme.* It was possibly the weirdest thing she'd ever seen. The French couple fought, then suddenly broke into a tuneless song, then went dancing down the streets. None of it made much sense, but she loved the bright, vibrant colors and the air of playfulness permeating the story.

Then something caught in Cassidy's throat. It wasn't a piece of popcorn—she hadn't had one bite all night. It wasn't gum or any other food-type product. It was air, of all things. Cassidy was feeling like an asthmatic in the peak of pollen season. Strangely enough, this little brush with hyperventilation started the moment the French couple began to take their clothes off while walking down a long stretch of beach.

Cassidy shuddered. Not that they were ugly or disfigured or anything. The French man was actually quite gorgeous, and the woman was very easy on the eyes too. But she was sitting there with Zach—her TA—*watching naked people*! As soon as the man and woman began to hungrily kiss each other, Cassidy's nerves went into overdrive. This was insanity. How was she supposed to remain cool and collected when the sight of full frontal nudity and the sound of lip smacking was reverberating all around her? There was only one thing to do—cover her eyes. She knew this would make her look like a little kid, but she didn't feel like she had any choice. If she didn't, her esophagus would close up and she would pass out and never get to see the ending. She had begun to bring her hands up to her eyes when she inadvertently knocked against Zach's arm in the process.

"Sorry," she whispered, beginning to move her arm away.

"No." Zach placed his hand over hers, sending electric shocks flying up her arm. "I'm sorry. I totally forgot this scene was in here. Do you want to leave?"

That was all she needed to feel better. The second she felt his touch, it was as if he'd made every ounce of discomfort vanish. And before she knew it, the couple were fully clothed again and drinking espresso at a café.

"That's okay. I'm fine," Cassidy replied breathlessly.

When he moved his hand away, she could still feel the warmth of his palm imprinted like a tattoo. As he settled deeper into his seat, his forearm touched hers and stayed there. Her skin felt hypersensitive to the contrast between the soft, ribbed material of his T-shirt and the smooth skin underneath, and the closeness made her dizzy. Could Zach hear the measured, deliberate pattern of her breath? She glanced sideways at him and he caught her eye and smiled, raising his eyebrow toward the screen as if to ask if she were enjoying the movie. She nodded slightly and looked ahead again, trying to seem as fascinated by the actors as she was by him. She knew she should probably move her arm, but would that seem too obvious? She didn't want Zach to know how aware she was of his proximity and the way it was making her feel inside. Cassidy was embarrassed to admit it even to herself, but just being next to him in this completely casual way was turning her on.

Zach shifted again, brushing his arm against hers, and a shiver went through her body.

"You sure you're all right?" he whispered in her ear.

"Yeah," she whispered back, finally moving her arm away to cross it in front of her chest. "Just a little cold."

Which sounded ludicrous because the theater was perfectly climate-controlled.

"I could go ask them to turn down the AC or something."

"No, really. Don't worry about it," she assured him.

The elderly woman behind them leaned forward and shushed them loudly, sending spittle spraying over the backs of their necks. They simultaneously put their hands over their mouths, suppressing giggles, and returned their attention to the screen, where the French couple was crying and saying good-bye.

*　　*　　*

"What'd you think?" Zach asked, turning to her when it was over. His eyes were bright with expectation.

"It was great!" Cassidy gushed, not wanting him to know how confused she'd been by the plot or how freaked out she'd been by the gratuitous exposing of flesh. Maybe it was the kind of thing you understood after you'd been in college for a year or two. Just the thought of that made Cassidy feel unsophisticated and stupid.

Zach smirked as they got up from their seats and made their way out into the warm, humid night. "It doesn't really make much sense, does it?" he asked.

"Nope." Cassidy shook her head, laughing. "Not a bit."

She was surprised that she didn't feel more embarrassed when she admitted that. Actually, Zach seemed happy she was so honest.

"This is the third time I've seen it and I'm still trying to figure out why the woman gives the guy a glass turtle," Zach said.

Since she hadn't scared him off yet, Cassidy decided to make her own observation of the movie. She never really did this because the thought of someone not understanding her always made her self-conscious, but Zach's open-mindedness and his friendly face put her at ease.

"I thought the turtle might be a symbol," Cassidy

mused. "Like she was trying to tell the guy she wanted to take it slow and let their relationship grow."

Zach raised an eyebrow. "Wow, I never quite looked at it that way before."

Cassidy felt so encouraged that she spoke up again. "It also makes sense when you think about how quickly the camera was moving around. Maybe that was the man's point of view, you know? Everything was rushed and frantic—" She stopped abruptly when she saw Zach's small grin transform into a wide smile. "I'm rambling, aren't I?"

His grin stayed put. "You really are an artist, you know that?" he asked. "I wish you'd stop saying you're not. It's obvious from the way you see things. You have an artist's eye."

"Maybe," Cassidy mumbled, looking at the ground.

"Well, you like to draw, right?" Zach asked. "How does drawing make you feel?"

Cassidy had to stop and think about that one. Nobody had ever asked her much about her art before. Larissa thought it was cute, but was mostly only interested in the pictures she was in. As for Eric, he was supportive of her art, but he always called it "a hobby," which made it seem like he didn't think what she did was important. Actually, Cassidy couldn't help but wonder where Eric was at that very moment. Probably out with his friends at a beach party, checking his phone every five minutes and waiting for her to call him and tell him that she really missed him. Her stomach cramped up when she thought of how she'd lied to him earlier, but the tension disappeared when she met Zach's inquisitive gaze. In fact, she was exhilarated by it.

"When I draw, I feel safe," she said finally. "Like I don't have to worry about anything. I can just be alone with the page and my pens and it's like I'm finally me."

"I know exactly what you mean," Zach said. "I'm a writer myself, and that's how I feel when I get lost in my imagination. It's like there are all these little voices in my head when I begin, and slowly they all leave the room one by one. Finally my own voice leaves the room, and that's when the magic happens."

Cassidy breathed in deeply. "That's such a perfect way of putting it."

I could never have this kind of conversation with Eric, she thought sadly. It really hurt her physically to feel that way.

"So are you going to art school after you graduate?" Zach asked.

"I don't know." She had never really thought about it.

"Well, you should," Zach said firmly. "If that's your passion, you should follow it."

"It's not really my *passion,*" Cassidy began, knowing even as the words left her mouth that they weren't true. A passion was something you lived for, and as much as she loved her friends and enjoyed school, she *lived* for drawing.

"I get the feeling that you're pretty into it," Zach said, as if reading her mind.

"Okay, I am," Cassidy said.

"Well, you should be true to yourself and do what makes you happy," Zach said.

Even though it sounded like the simplest thing in the world, Cassidy realized she had never seen it that way before. It seemed like nobody had ever asked her what *she* was interested in. Her parents just assumed she wanted to follow the path they had set for her, with the special programs and the studies abroad and the ultra-organized lifestyle. And Larissa always acted like Cassidy would be into whatever she wanted to do, and Eric was such a live-in-the-now kind of guy that he'd never even mentioned what would happen after high school. That was what made Zach different: the way he seemed to bring Cassidy out of her shell long enough for her to realize what *she* wanted.

"Maybe I'll look into art school," Cassidy said, high on the mingling smells of summer and the dizzying prospect of going to college for something she loved. "Do you know which ones are good?"

Zach was about to answer when Cassidy caught sight of several familiar figures emerging from a Thai bistro across the street. One had dreadlocks, one was Japanese, and one was lanky with long red hair and a tiny miniskirt. Cassidy's heart rate doubled as she realized she was looking at Dina, Fumiko, and Larissa, who would certainly ask her a zillion questions about why she was coming out of a movie theater with a guy who was absolutely, positively not Eric. She glanced around wildly for somewhere she could go to avoid them, but it was already too late. Larissa rushed toward her, wrapping her in a giant hug.

"Hey, girl!" Larissa squealed, noisily air-kissing both of her cheeks.

Cassidy winced. Larissa *never* air-kissed, nor did she usually spend her time hanging out in Santa Monica. It was just Cassidy's twisted kind of luck that they'd run into each other here tonight.

"Wow, you look hot!" Larissa continued. "Wasn't I right when I told you to get that top?"

"I guess so," Cassidy mumbled, beginning to blush. The last thing she wanted was for Larissa to make a bad impression on Zach. He and Cassidy were definitely connecting, and she was fearful that one snide comment from Larissa about how Cassidy used to pee her pants when she got tickled might wreck all the respect she'd seemingly established tonight.

Fumiko, Dina, and the rest of their group caught up to Larissa. "Hey, Cassidy," Fumiko said. "How's summer school?"

"Much better than expected," Cassidy said. As soon as the words were out of her mouth, she hiccuped. *Try not to be a total moron, Cass.* "In fact, this is my TA, Zach."

She and Larissa made quick introductions, all of them standing in a circle on the sidewalk as people flowed around them. "So hey," Dina said. "We're all heading to this new club a couple of blocks from here. Want to come with?"

Cassidy snuck a sideways glance at Zach, who looked at her and shrugged.

"Come on, you *have* to," Larissa pleaded. "Bar Copa supposedly has the best dance music in Santa Monica."

Cassidy didn't want to hear the best dance music in Santa Monica. She wanted to keep talking to Zach, out in the quiet night, just the two of them. But she realized being alone with Zach might be treading on dangerous ground. At least with Larissa around, she'd be less likely to do something she'd regret, like tackle Zach in his car and kiss him senseless. Besides, she had barely hung out with Larissa in the last week or so, and it would be nice to get in some best-friend time. Maybe Larissa could even help her figure out what to do about the Zach situation. Not that there was much to do except obsess about him secretly, of course.

"Sure, that sounds great," she said. "Let's do it."

As Dina led them down Montana Avenue, Larissa pulled Cassidy aside so the two of them were out of earshot of the rest of the group.

"So what gives?" she whispered. "Are you sneaking this guy behind Eric's back?"

Cassidy rolled her eyes. "It's unlike you to be so subtle, Larissa."

"I'm just curious, hon. You did 911 me and everything."

"Right, well, I told you how my teacher's all into this experiential education crap," Cassidy explained. "So she wanted us to go see this movie, and there's a quiz on it Monday."

Larissa didn't appear to be convinced. "Your homework is your 911?"

Cassidy crossed her arms in front of her chest and scowled.

"Right, you're a nerd. That makes sense," Larissa conceded. "But let's talk about the more interesting part of this experimental educational thingy. Like how you've got the sexiest TA ever." Larissa's voice rose the way it always did when she got excited about something. Cassidy glanced toward Zach, but he was already in an animated conversation with Fumiko, Dina, and their two friends. Cassidy could barely believe he'd been as shy as she was just a couple of years before.

"You really think he's sexy?" Cassidy lowered her voice so that Zach wouldn't be able to hear her.

"Um, does Mary-Kate Olsen shoot up in between her toes?" Larissa asked sarcastically. "Cass, I know you love Eric to pieces, but you've got eyes too, right? Did you *really* not notice how hot Zach is?"

"No, I didn't," Cassidy lied through her teeth for the second time that day.

"Is he single?" Larissa asked. "Can I hit on him, or would that be icky since he's your TA?"

Cassidy tried to quell a major heart palpitation. "I'm not sure."

"Whatever. Like it matters," Larissa replied as she shifted her boobs for maximum cleavage. "You sure you don't mind if I—"

"You can do whatever you want," Cassidy blurted. But that wasn't what she'd wanted to say at all. She just couldn't bear to hear Larissa going on and on about Zach anymore, and if she'd said that making a move on him would make her uncomfortable, Larissa would know the truth.

Cassidy was absolutely smitten.

"Cool." Larissa wiggled her eyebrows. "Wish me luck!" She bounced off toward Zach, leaving Cassidy walking by herself and feeling about as important as a dusty sock that had fallen under the bed. Her stomach wrenched again as Larissa slid into step beside Zach and said something that made him laugh. When he responded, Larissa threw back her head and shook out her hair, which shimmered briefly as they passed under a streetlight before falling back into shadow.

The image of Zach and Larissa enjoying each other's company made her squirm inside. Cassidy couldn't believe how jealous she was getting over someone who wasn't even her boyfriend. Sometimes she got a little cagey when Eric talked to other girls, but it never got to the point of physical pain. She slowed down, falling even farther behind the rest of the group. She took deep breaths, hoping that later on she wouldn't have a good reason to want to close her eyes.

Chapter Nine

W e're here!" Fumiko announced, stopping at an unmarked black metal door in a nondescript building on Main Street in Santa Monica. Cassidy could hear muffled music thumping through the walls of Bar Copa. After Fumiko said something about them all being on a list, Cassidy followed the group inside and down a flight of narrow metal stairs, the music growing louder and louder as they descended. Cassidy could hear hip-hop beats layered on top of each other, could smell the sweat of bodies crushed together before her group was all the way downstairs. The long, narrow room was barely lit, so that the people writhing on the dance floor were mere shadows flickering in the red lighting. She slid into an empty purple velvet chair in the corner, watching as Larissa followed Zach to the bar, gesturing animatedly the whole way.

What was up with Larissa's newfound ability to pretend Cassidy didn't exist? She tapped her foot against the floor, watching the DJ flip a record in the air and land it precisely in the center of the turntable, snapping his fingers casually along with music. A long-haired guy in a tight black tank top sat next to him on a metal chair, a drum between his legs. He drummed another layer on top of the beat, his hands flying over the drum's tight skin. Cassidy realized she was tapping her foot to the beat, even nodding a little. Larissa had been right. The music *was* pretty good. Still, a decent beat wasn't enough to keep her sitting in the corner of some bar all night while Zach flirted with her best friend. If Larissa thought Cassidy was going to play Invisible Girl again, she was dead wrong.

Cassidy had just decided to split when Zach materialized in front of her, a drink sweating in each hand.

"I got you a Red Bull," he said. "Wasn't sure what you wanted, but these are fun when you're dancing. It's a big energy rush."

"Thanks." Cassidy took the drink, appreciating how thoughtful Zach was. She looked around for Larissa, but she was still by the bar, winking at the bartender as she handed him a five and slid her lips over the straw in her drink.

"You want to dance?" Zach asked.

"I'm not much of a dancer," she admitted shyly.

"I'm not much of a dancer either."

"So we can both suck together?"

"We can have a contest," Zach joked, taking her hand and leading her through the tangle of bodies to the middle of the dance floor. "Whoever sucks less has to buy the other person a drink."

Cassidy laughed and sipped her Red Bull, sinking into the beat like a warm bath and then looking up to see Zach smiling at her. She couldn't believe how easy he was to dance with. Zach didn't suck nearly as bad as he'd claimed. He just moved easily to the beat, his eyes locked onto hers and the trace of a grin spreading across his face.

Something about being there with Zach made her forget there were other people around her. The music flowed through her, coming out through her feet and hands, shaking her body in ways she hadn't known before. She looked at her drink, realized it was empty, and danced over to the wall to put it down on a table before spinning back to Zach, taking the hand he offered her and letting him pull her in close. She was near enough to smell him—a mix of soap, old books, and sweat—and she thought dizzily that it was the sexiest smell in the world.

"You don't suck at all!" Zach laughed over the music. "You owe me a drink!"

"Maybe later." Cassidy smiled. She closed her eyes and swayed back and forth, savoring the electric currents zooming between them. Dancing with Eric had never felt this close or sexy. She should stop, she realized. Things could get out of hand, and she wasn't sure she could deal with the consequences of grabbing Zach by his white T-shirt and pulling him in for a warm, electric kiss.

"So what do you think of the place?" she asked, stepping back a little. Maybe if she got them on another topic, she'd be able to cool down. As it was, being so near him made her feel like she was about to explode.

"It's great," Zach replied. "Just like Larissa promised. She kind of reminds me of Jimmy, my best friend in high school. He was always going a hundred miles a minute too."

"Yeah, she's a little wild," Cassidy admitted.

"Let me guess," Zach said. "You're the quiet one who's always by her side?"

Cassidy was glad the club was too dark for him to see her blushing.

"I'm just kind of shy," she said.

Zach drew her in closer, his arms around her waist. "It's funny," he said. "You don't seem shy to me at all."

His eyes gleamed in the candlelight, a slight smile playing on the corners of his mouth. He began to bend his head toward her and she could feel the heat between them. Cassidy was both scared and excited at the thought of him kissing her, but her guilt kicked in before anything mind-blowing happened.

"I have to go to the bathroom." She wriggled away and dodged through the crowd. She needed to talk to Larissa like *whoa!* Her life was spiraling out of control very quickly, and she hoped Larissa would be able to talk some sense into her before she did something she'd seriously regret.

"Bathroom," she commanded, dragging Larissa off her bar stool and toward the door with the skirted figure on the outside.

"So what's up?" Larissa asked once they were safe under the fluorescent overhead lighting. She rummaged in her oversize bag for her Lancôme bronzer and momentarily disappeared in a puffy glittering cloud. Cassidy watched her and tried to compose herself. She realized she didn't even know where to begin.

"They're pretty cool, aren't they?" Larissa asked, taking advantage of the silence.

"Cool?" Cassidy said. She had no idea what Larissa was talking about. Who were "they"?

"Fumiko and Dina's friends," Larissa continued. "That guy Toby with the shaved head—did you know he's a professional graffiti artist? And then Mary-Jane, who won't tell me what she does, but I bet it's something *really* nasty. Do you think she's a dominatrix? She has that vibe. And, like, who actually names their kid *Mary-Jane*?"

Cassidy couldn't have picked Toby or Mary-Jane out of a police lineup. All she could think about was Zach's face swimming close to hers, the look in his eyes, and that tiny smile.

"I guess so," Cassidy said. "I didn't talk to them much yet."

"You really should," Larissa said. "I mean, Mary-Jane is fab, but Toby is just . . . amazing. He used to live in San Francisco and build sets. He's totally ripped too. You should check out his biceps if you get a chance."

Cassidy tried to picture Toby in her mind, but she couldn't help seeing Zach—and, of course, Eric, who would be completely heartbroken if he knew where she was, and who she was with, and how she was starting to feel.

"Is he that bald guy?" she asked.

"He's not bald; he just shaves his head," Larissa said. "I mean, he's like in his early twenties—how could he be bald? You're really out of it tonight, Cass. I can't believe I introduced you to Toby and you can barely remember who he is."

"I'm sorry," Cassidy said. She suddenly felt drained, as if in between wanting Zach and worrying about Eric, she'd expended her allotment of energy for the night. "I guess I'm just a little nervous about the quiz and everything."

Larissa shrugged. "So go home and study," she said, sounding put out. "I'm going to stay here, and then Dina's having an after party at her place since we don't have to open the store until noon tomorrow."

Cassidy waited for Larissa to invite her along like she

always did when there was a party, but Larissa just headed for the door.

"Come on," she said. "They're going to think we drowned in here."

"Wait!" Cassidy said. Larissa paused, her hand on the doorknob.

"What?" she asked.

"What do you think of Zach?"

"He's okay, whatever," Larissa said. "I asked him if he wanted my number, but he said he was interested in someone else."

She pushed through the door and back to her friends, and Cassidy followed slowly, her head spinning. He'd said he was interested in somebody, but he couldn't be talking about her, could he? Cassidy's muscles tensed up the moment she approached the dance floor and saw Zach waiting patiently for her. He stretched out his hand, beckoning her to join him once more. She took a deep breath and walked forward, hoping that she was the one, yet she was almost frightened of what was to come.

*   *   *

Cassidy pulled into her driveway and snuck quietly into her house. Once she got to her room, she pulled out her cell phone and noticed the red light on top was blinking. Just as she was flopping onto her bed to check her messages, her phone rang again—the special 50 Cent ring tone she'd set just for Eric. She hesitated a moment before steeling herself and hitting Talk.

"Sweetie!" His voice was riddled with a combination of anxiety and relief. "I tried calling you three times, and when you didn't pick up, I swung by your place to see if you were okay. But your parents said you went out. I thought you had to study for some test?"

"I'm sorry," Cassidy said. *More sorry than you could ever know.* "I forgot to tell you, our homework was to go see this movie, and then I ran into Larissa afterward and we ended up going out dancing."

"And you didn't invite me?"

Cassidy knew she couldn't blame Eric for being suspicious this time. "Well, I left my cell at home and . . . and Larissa's couldn't get a signal. Otherwise I would have called, seriously."

Great. There's lie number 4.

"Well, it would have been nice to see you," Eric said. "It seems like we're spending less and less time together. You don't have someone stashed on the side, do you?"

She swallowed hard. Even though technically nothing had happened between her and Zach, the fact that Cassidy was fantasizing about him made her feel very remorseful. Still, she couldn't bring herself to tell Eric that she felt herself slipping away from him.

"Of course not," she replied.

"Good. So how about spending some quality time tomorrow night when I get off work?"

Cassidy tried to muster up a heap of enthusiasm. "Sounds great." She hoped it sounded convincing.

"Cool." Fortunately Eric sounded like his normal, happy-go-lucky self. "See you tomorrow, sweetie."

"Good night," Cassidy said, flipping her phone shut.

She rolled over and lay on her back. She could still see Zach's face just inches from hers and thought she might be able to call up his smell in her memory if she tried hard enough. She returned her cell to its cradle, got undressed, and crawled into bed. She glanced at a framed photo on her nightstand. It was of her and Eric rock climbing at Zuma Beach. Cassidy smiled at the sight of her and Eric dangling from two ropes, waving at Larissa, who had taken the picture. She could feel a wave of sorrow come over her as she turned off the light, but it left her when she curled up under the sheets and shut her eyes. She played the scene from the dance floor over and over again in her head. Each time, Zach's lips got closer to hers. When she finally fell asleep, they were touching, and their imaginary kiss lingered on all night in her dreams.

Chapter Ten

Dear Cassidy,

Thanks for your letter. I think it saved my life. It's great to hear that you still get to do fun things like seeing movies and going out dancing. Those simple pleasures feel like distant memories to me in my mosquito-ridden mountaintop prison. Your TA sounds cool, and I think his advice about art school is right on. As for Eric being jealous, I have one word for you: DUH! Of course, he's jealous, Cass. He's got this amazing girlfriend and he knows it's just a matter of time before she realizes how great she is and hitches a ride to "I'm a sexy independent *artist"-ville and leaves him in the dust. Seriously, though, if you keep this Zach guy a secret, it's going to bite you in the ass eventually. That's how secrets are.*

Things at Camp Crackhead keep getting worse. Lloyd got his little brother to smuggle in a bunch of Ritalin over Parents Weekend, and the other night everyone in my bunk took it—except for me, of course. They totally tried to get me to, but there is no way I'm touching any kind of controlled substance if it's going to make me end up like these losers. At the rate things are going, I'm half afraid to take aspirin when I get a headache.

So anyway, they crushed up all this Ritalin and snorted it after lights-out the other night, and I thought the roof was going to fly off our bunk. Everyone started bouncing off the walls. This guy Peter was slurping ketchup packets from the cafeteria and shouting, "I am Superdog!" Then Lloyd and a bunch of his cronies told me that if I didn't reenact the light saber fight between Anakin Skywalker and Obi-Wan Kenobi in Revenge of the Sith, they would throw me down the can in the outhouse. You're going to think I'm totally lame, but did I mention Lloyd is three hundred pounds? Want to know another secret about boys? We may pretend to be macho, but we'll seriously do anything we can to prevent our teeth from getting knocked out.

Anyway, it's too bad you missed it because there is no way I'm repeating that performance!

Cassidy, I'm worried for my life and sanity. Seriously. If you don't hear from me in a week, call the police. I would take a lifetime of French classes over this. I never thought I'd say this, but I can't wait for fall.

Oh, one last thing: good luck with the whole TA thing. Don't worry—I won't tell Eric. It'll be our little secret. . . .

Cheers,

Joe

PS I've been honing my Pictionary skills. Be afraid. Be very afraid.

"We're almost there, crickets!" Madame Briand called over her shoulder to the twenty students trekking wearily behind her. Of all the places Cassidy would have thought of going to for a French field trip, the Los Angeles Zoo was hardly one of them. But Madame Briand was so loopy, there was no telling what she might consider educational.

"Look, it's your cousin," Benjy said, pointing to an ape picking fleas off his scalp and popping them into his mouth.

"I thought it was your twin brother," Cassidy shot back. "Identical, naturally."

"Girl's getting lippy!" Benjy said. He seemed almost pleased with her retort.

"Ici, ici!" Madame Briand pushed open the door to a pavilion labeled BIRD SANCTUARY. A zoo employee in a small round hat met them inside. His tan uniform shirt drooped on his cadaverous frame, and a pair of round steel-rimmed glasses slipped perpetually down the length of his beak-like nose. A patch sewn on the front of his uniform read MORRIS: BIRD EXPERT.

"Hello," he said to the class.

"Bonjour!" Cecilia twittered.

"Morris is going to tell us about a very special bird," Madame Briand announced.

"Well, yes," Morris began in a nasal drawl. "I suppose it's particularly special for all you Francophiles. You see that little guy over there?"

The class dutifully followed his pointing finger with their eyes. In a building full of brilliant plumage, he seemed to be indicating a small, brown, and utterly ordinary bird. It looked like one of the sparrows that pecked at Cassidy's lawn and drove their gardener crazy.

"That there's a Corsican nuthatch." For a moment, Morris seemed almost happy. "It's only been spotted in France—in Corsica, off the southern coast, to be exact."

Madame Briand literally clapped with joy.

"Mon Dieu!" Cecilia squealed. Benjy rolled his eyes and made quiet gagging sounds.

"It's thought that the Corsican nuthatch is evolved

from the Aegean crested nuthatch," Morris droned on. "Which in Darwinian theory must have migrated across the continent in . . ."

Already bored, Cassidy wandered to the other side of the sanctuary, where a pair of ducks glided happily on the surface of a small pond, occasionally going bottoms up in search of a meal.

"Quack," someone whispered in her ear. A thrill coursed through her body when she realized it was Zach.

"Who, Morris or the ducks?" she whispered back.

"Both." He laughed. "Are you as bored as I am?"

"That's why I'm over here," she said. "I was starting to become comatose."

"Well, maybe that bird is related to Madame Briand," Zach whispered. "It's a Corsican nuthatch, and she's a Quebecois nut."

Out of the corner of her eye, Cassidy could see the rest of the class exiting the bird sanctuary. She knew she should say something but couldn't bring herself to lose the few precious minutes this would give her alone with Zach. It had been two weeks since they'd had their kinda, sorta date and they hadn't had too much time alone together since.

"I think she's getting nuttier," Cassidy said. "Since when does a visit to the Los Angeles Zoo equal learning French?"

"Are you really complaining about getting out of the classroom and seeing cute animals on a beautiful day?" Zach asked playfully. The way he smiled made Cassidy's stomach tighten, and she had to remind herself to think about Eric and the nice thing he did the other day. But once she caught a glimpse of Zach's cute butt, she could barely remember her zip code.

"We should really go find the rest of the class," she said. "I don't want to get you in trouble." *Or me,* she thought. *Trouble with a capital* T.

"You're right. Although I doubt anyone would miss us." Zach headed toward the door. They emerged into a sunlit plaza between several pavilions. A young mother strolled by pushing a carriage, and a group of elderly tourists doddered by in orthopedic shoes, but the rest of their class seemed to have disappeared.

"Where do you think they went?" Cassidy asked.

"Knowing Madame Briand, they've probably boarded a hot-air balloon to Paris by now," Zach joked.

Cassidy laughed in spite of herself. Zach could be so funny and charming. *But so can Eric,* she thought diplomatically. *You know . . .* Eric? *Your boyfriend?* She checked out Zach's rear end again. *Right, Eric. That guy who probably loves you but hasn't said it after two years.*

She shook her head and refocused her attention on the situation at hand. She pointed toward the Hidden Jungle pavilion. "Let's try that one."

As they pushed aside the long plastic strips hanging in the doorway, Cassidy had to pause to let her eyes adjust to the darkness. Almost immediately, sweat began to bead on her forehead. Lush greenery poked through the net overhanging the wooden path that led through the pavilion, and small, lighted signs informed them about what might be lurking in the darkness.

"Wow," Cassidy said.

"This reminds me of South America." Zach sighed. "Have you ever been?"

Cassidy was astounded. Zach had seen so many things that she hadn't, and every time she learned of some exotic place he'd traveled to, he became more and more interesting to her.

"No, not yet," she replied.

"I like that you said 'not yet.' I had a feeling that there was an explorer inside you too."

Cassidy got so flustered by how his gaze was steadily fixed on her face that she changed the subject. "I guess they're somewhere else," she said. "It's way too quiet for Madame Briand and Cecilia to both be in here."

"Or maybe they got eaten by *that*." Zach pointed at a sign picturing a black leopard.

Cassidy peered through the rain forest, looking for the leopard, but could only see more ferns. She caught a quick, darting movement out of the corner of her eye and her heart thudded in her chest, but when she whirled to face it, all she saw was a blue-tailed skunk racing up the trunk of a palm tree.

"Don't be scared," Zach whispered.

She wasn't sure if he meant of him or the leopard.

"Me? Never." Cassidy's heart was beating double time. Zach was merely two feet away from her, and the way his hair was getting damp from the humidity was making her imagine him in the shower. . . .

"I think it's there," Zach said, pointing over her shoulder. She turned and saw two small, silvery disks glinting from behind a low-hanging plant. A pair of eyes. They were staring at her deeply, and she was rendered motionless. She wasn't terrified by it at all. In fact, she was invigorated and thrilled at being in direct contact with something that was so much out of her world. But she didn't feel like an outsider for once. It was as if this animal were telling her to come closer, inviting her into its lair. The only thing that stood between them was this thick wall of glass. She wished that it would just melt away so that she could get closer and find out what would happen next.

"It's amazing, isn't it?" Zach asked softly. "That something so beautiful would want to stay hidden."

Cassidy knew that if she turned around, she'd be close enough to kiss him. "Maybe it's for protection."

"From what?"

"I don't know." Her voice was so faint, she wasn't even sure she'd said anything.

"What?" he asked again.

Cassidy spun around and Zach was within reach. She looked him right in the eyes, just as the leopard had done to her. She took a step toward him. Zach put his hand on her shoulder as if to stop her, and his touch burned through the fabric of her shirt and into her skin. Her arms seemed to wrap around his back naturally as she breathed in his sexy scent of Ivory and books, squeezing him as if he might turn into a cloud of vapor and disappear at any moment. Energy coursed through her body, pooling in the space below her stomach. She knew she should let go right away or else she would do something that would ruin everything between her and Eric forever.

But she closed her eyes and just felt everything—the sweat rolling down her cheeks, his lips brushing hers, the heat radiating from his body as he drew her in closer, their tongues slowly meeting as his hands roamed over her back.

Kissing Zach was like nothing she'd ever experienced. It was such a far cry from the fun, comforting kisses she shared with Eric. Zach's mouth moved slowly and passionately. Cassidy felt herself starting to quiver. She had never wanted anyone so badly in her life.

"Oh, my!"

Cassidy leapt back and found herself face-to-face with two elderly ladies, both wearing floral dresses and orthopedic shoes.

"Well, this really *is* the jungle pavilion, isn't it!" one of them said. The other suppressed a giggle.

Cassidy's hand flew to her mouth. She looked quickly at Zach, whose eyes were glazed with shock, before running away through the pavilion, ferns and netting brushing her bare arms, her footsteps pounding on the slatted wooden pathway. She pushed open the door under a glowing Exit sign and kept running, stumbling blindly in the summer light, not stopping until she'd reached the parking lot and was safe in her mom's old Volvo. She slammed the door shut behind her and locked it for good measure, pulling her knees up to her chest and resting her head between them. She was shaking and couldn't seem to stop.

She tried to think if there was a chapter in Sandra Jones's book about what to do when you cheated on your boyfriend of two years with a guy you barely knew—and enjoyed it—but her mind went blank, except for every detail about that kiss. She could still feel the imprint of his chest on hers, the slight sting where his stubble had brushed her cheek. She was a horrible person. That's all there was to it. Nothing she could do would ever make up for what had just happened.

She reached into her purse and pulled out her cell, speed-dialing Larissa's number and clenching her teeth through two endless rings.

"Hey, Cass," Larissa said, picking up the phone. "What's up?"

"I'm . . . Well, we just went to the zoo. . . ." Cassidy didn't even know where to begin.

"The zoo?" Larissa asked. "No, make it a little shorter."

"What?!" Cassidy asked. Was Larissa really telling her to hurry up?

"Not you," Larissa said. "Dina. We're working on the collection." Her voice grew muffled. "It's Cassidy. Yeah, definitely alligator print."

"Larissa, I . . . I don't know what to do. . . ."

"Oh, Dina says hi. No, even shorter than that. Legs are *in* this season! Don't know what to do about what?"

Cassidy was still trembling and wondering if she should even tell anyone about this. Once she did, it all became real. She was only able to stammer out a few fragments of sentences. "Well, things just got totally out of hand with Zach. And I really like him, but I'm still with Eric and I . . ."

"I'm sorry, can you repeat that?" Larissa asked. "Dina was just explaining something and I kind of got distracted."

"That's a first," Cassidy said sarcastically.

Larissa sighed in frustration. "What crawled into your panties and died?"

"You know what? Forget it," Cassidy said. "You're not even paying attention to me."

"Okay, cool," Larissa said so amiably that Cassidy was pretty sure she was either talking to someone else or hadn't heard what she'd said.

"Good-bye, Larissa," Cassidy said icily.

"Oh, bye, hon," she replied cheerfully. "Listen, call me later; I'll be less distracted. Promise!" She made a kissy noise into the receiver before hanging up.

Cassidy snapped her phone shut with disgust. Could things be worse? She was a cheat, her best friend was being a total flake, and she'd have to see Zach again in class the next day. How could she face him after what had just happened? For that matter, how could she face *Eric*? She was sure that the moment she saw him, he'd know, and she couldn't bear the thought of hurting him. Just the thought of his sweet, trusting smile made her feel sick with guilt.

Cassidy started the engine but quickly turned it off again. There was no way she could drive—her eyes were too full of tears.

Chapter Eleven

It was Monday morning and Zach was looking at her again. It seemed like every time she glanced up from the grammar quiz she was supposedly taking (and would probably fail miserably), her eyes caught his. She glanced back down at the page. How was she supposed to conjugate *avoir* with the sexiest guy in the universe sitting twenty feet away? How could she concentrate on *anything* when they had shared this fantastically erotic moment and they'd barely acknowledged it? If this stuff was the norm in France, Cassidy wasn't sure if she ever wanted to visit her aunt Geraldine.

She had to remind herself that she was no longer allowed to think of Zach as sexy. After a long weekend of isolation, crying, and soul-searching, she'd decided that there would be no more kisses: Eric was her boyfriend, and Zach was just her TA. As she'd waited for the coffee to brew in the empty kitchen before she left for school that morning, Cassidy had made a vow to re-dedicate herself to Eric. After all, their second anniversary was coming up, and it just might be her chance to hear the three little words she'd been waiting for. She'd come to the conclusion that hearing those sentiments from Eric would change everything. Her feelings for Zach would just evapo-rate into the air and her life would go back to normal. She'd convinced herself that the reason she was so enamored with Zach was because there was this big thing missing with Eric, and once she got it, she'd stop thinking about Zach in nothing but his boxers.

As she sat at her desk, Cassidy tried to lose herself in the fantasy of her first time with Eric: there'd be an expensive hotel room, satin sheets, champagne, and candlelight. But Zach kept edging his way into the scene and pushing Eric right out the window. While thinking about fooling around with Eric gave her a warm, vague sense of pleasure, every time she recalled the kiss with Zach at the zoo, a jolt of pure lust made her stomach flip. She wished she could just turn off her attraction to Zach so maybe she could get a moment of peace. This was how people felt about serious addictions. She won-dered if they had a Camp Crackhead somewhere for girls who just couldn't get over boys.

"Cinq minutes!" Madame Briand cried from the front of the room. Cassidy sighed and leaned over her quiz, trying vainly to push both Eric and Zach out of her mind. *Avoir* meant "to have." Why couldn't she just have both?

She struggled to focus on the quiz in front of her, wishing her parents had never heard of the California International Language and Culture Institute. Then she wouldn't have gotten into this whole mess in the first place. Then she could have worked at Seersucker with Larissa and had sex with Eric on their second anniversary without any second thoughts. Maybe they'd have stayed together forever and she'd go through life without ever knowing that a kiss could make you feel like you'd been kicked in the stomach with a Manolo Blahnik stiletto heel.

"Arrêtes!" Madame Briand cried, and Cassidy struggled to fill in the rest of the answers, finally cutting her mind off from every thought but verb tense as she watched her pen fly over the bottom of the page.

She looked up to see Zach standing over her, waiting to collect her paper. His face was expressionless, but his eyes seemed very stormy and brooding. She felt her face go scarlet and quickly looked down at the marks someone had scratched into her desk: MH + CW = < 3. She wondered how long she and Zach were going to avoid each other. A few days? A few weeks? Forever? She was just so confused inside. She was scared that if they were alone again, she would leap on him, rip off all his clothes, and do something with him that would change her whole life irreversibly. At the same time, she was just as scared at the thought of that never happening at all.

Cassidy looked up again to see Zach shuffling away and moving on to the next student. The clock on the wall ticked loudly past 4:31 P.M., so she hurriedly stuffed her textbook and pen into her bag. She brushed past him out the door, trying to ignore the tiny catch in her heartbeat as she glanced briefly back at the golden curve of his neck. She reminded herself not to think about how sexy Zach was, especially because she was on her way to meet her boyfriend.

*   *   *

Cassidy arrived at Point Dume just in time to see Eric dragging two surfboards up from the water. One was his: she'd recognize those familiar red-and-blue flames any-where. But the other must belong to the blonde girl in the tiny purple string bikini walking alongside him on the sand, flipping her hair back and turning her tiny but-ton nose toward him as she laughed at something he had said. Cassidy felt the back of her neck knot with distrust when she saw the way Eric smiled at the girl. Then she caught herself. Who was *she* to be distrustful when she'd had a hot zoological make-out session with her TA just the day before?

Still, Cassidy couldn't help but feel like this girl was invading her territory and she had to protect it somehow. She quickly slipped off her shoes and ran down the beach, throwing her arms around Eric and squeezing him tight. She felt his wet board suit press up against her and inhaled the salty smell of his skin in hopes it would have the same effect on her as Zach's musty, bookish scent. As Eric laughed and picked her up off the ground, she surprised both of them by wrapping her legs around his waist and planting a big, fat kiss on his lips. *What the hell am I doing?* she thought. *This is a textbook Larissa move.*

Eric seemed surprised too. He held her at arm's length, laughing. "You've never greeted me like *that* before. I like it!"

Even though it seemed to make Eric happy, Cassidy felt so deflated. She'd thought that forcing herself to be more into Eric would make her thoughts of Zach go away, but it hadn't. When Cassidy slipped her arm around Eric's waist and rested her head on his shoulder, she secretly wished that she was at the beach with Zach. Luckily, Eric and the blond couldn't read her mind. The girl bit her lower lip and looked down at her pearly pink toenails as if she'd just been yelled at.

"This is Dee, one of my surfing students," Eric said.

"And Dee, this is Cassidy, my girlfriend." His face glowed with pride as they politely reached for each other's hands. Cassidy winced slightly as Dee's fingernails dug into the flesh of her palm.

"Yeah, listen, I have to run." Dee was obviously pissed that Cassidy had ruined her moment alone with Eric. "I'm going dancing at 14 Below tonight. The band is supposed to be really hot. Maybe I'll see you there?" She directed her last comment straight at Eric, but he just shrugged and slung his arm over Cassidy's shoulders.

"I dunno, Dee," he said. "We might show up, but I doubt it." He gave Cassidy a squeeze and a private smile. Dee sighed, picked up her surfboard, and trudged up the beach, her shoulders drooping like a beagle's ears.

"So what *do* you want to do?" Cassidy asked, almost disappointed that they weren't going to 14 Below. She'd been there a couple of times and liked the upbeat atmosphere. In fact, the live rock bands usually performed at such loud volumes, so if she went there with Eric she wouldn't be able to say much to him. And the less they talked, she thought, the less likely she'd be to blurt out what had happened with Zach.

"I don't care," Eric said, taking her hand and swinging it back and forth as they strolled toward the wooden shed where the surfers stored their equipment. "I'm just happy to be spending time with you."

"Yeah?" Cassidy said cagily. Was he implying that

she'd been "spending time" with someone else, or was she just being paranoid?

Most likely paranoid to the hundredth degree.

"I've missed you so much," Eric said emphatically. He swung open the door to the shed, and Cassidy breathed in the scent of surf wax and moldering rubber suits hung out to dry. She'd always imagined the shack was haunted, and had several sketches in her notebook of ghostly surfers emerging from it at midnight to ride the waves they'd lost their lives to. When she'd showed it to Eric, he'd patted her on the head and told her it was cute. Now she was contemplating what Zach would say if she showed him her sketchbook. Her heart began to float when she imagined him critiquing her work and asking her questions. The thought of it gave her the kind of adrenaline rush that Eric probably got when he surfed.

The door banged shut behind them, and Cassidy watched the muscles in Eric's back flex in the dim light as he carefully placed his board on a set of pegs drilled into the wall, nestling it among its fellow boards for the night. He ran his hand reverently along the smooth underside before turning to Cassidy and staring at her with the same affection. She couldn't help but think in that moment that maybe they were just on different wavelengths.

"What?" she asked. He'd been looking at her for too long, and she was starting to get creeped out. Was he trying to read the guilt in her face? Maybe he could see right through her.

"Nothing," he said, shaking his head as if coming out of a trance. "It's just that you're so beautiful, it still catches me off guard sometimes."

Cassidy forced a smile. She used to love hearing Eric tell her how she was beautiful, but now it felt like she didn't deserve the compliment.

"Seriously." Eric stepped toward her and took her face in his hands, lowering his head to kiss her gently on the lips. Cassidy begged herself to respond, but her lips felt like they'd been injected with novocaine, and she could barely manage to wrap her arms around his back. It didn't take long for Eric to get the hint and back off.

"You're mad at me, aren't you?" He pulled away and leaned against one of the sawhorses the surfers used to wax their boards.

She began to protest, but he wouldn't let her continue.

"I don't blame you," he said, lowering his head and fingering a stray thread that was coming loose from the waistband of his colorful shorts. "I've been a real dick lately. I'm sorry."

"No, you haven't!" *She* was the dick, not him!

"It's okay, I know I have," Eric said. "About the Joe thing and stuff like that. I've been thinking about it, and I realized I was just being paranoid. It's just that sometimes I get scared I'm going to lose you, you know?"

Cassidy's heart clenched. She could actually feel it squeezing inside her chest, growing smaller as she stared at a crack in the wall to avoid looking at Eric. It was exactly like Joe had said.

"Anyway, I'm really sorry," he continued. "I just . . . really care about you."

"You're not going to lose me," she said quietly, feeling her heart sink as soon as the words were out of her mouth. She tried desperately not to admit, even to herself, that Eric had probably lost her already. But it was too late.

She could feel that most of her was already gone.

Chapter Twelve

July 27

Hi Joe,

Thanks so much for your last letter. It was really sweet—exactly what I needed with how chaotic everything has been here. Not that it's so bad compared to how you have it, though. Those kids in your bunk sound nuts! Next time they try and force you to do silly impressions, let them know there's a five-foot-five spunky brunette back in Malibu just waiting to kick their butts.

On the other hand, maybe you shouldn't. Who knows what the repercussions might be?

Anyway, things are fine. Actually, that's a total lie. I'm just so confused about everything. Tonight is my two-year anniversary with Eric and I'm pretty sure he has something really special planned, and I can't figure out why I'm dreading it so much. Except that it might be because I think I'm starting to like someone else. I don't know. It's really freaky. It's like for the past two years, I've always thought Eric was The One, and now that it's coming time to prove it, I'm not sure that's how I feel anymore. Isn't that messed up? I keep thinking I'll wake up some morning and everything will be like it used to be. Or maybe I'm just going through some stage that all girls go through after they've been dating someone for two years. Maybe it's a secret that my fellow girls forgot to tell me about.

But I've blabbed on long enough. Larissa actually managed to clear a couple of hours in her schedule for her so-called best friend, and I can hear her car in the driveway right this moment.

Hope you haven't starved to death or gotten hooked on crack by the time you get this!

Speak to you soon,
C

Cassidy quickly folded the note in thirds, slipped it into an envelope, and scribbled the address of Camp Crackhead on the outside. She slid it between the pages of her sketchbook just as Larissa barged into her room, hair frizzing up around her head from the slight summer humidity and cheeks pink with excitement. Cassidy had never been so glad to see her best friend. For the past week or so, Larissa had been harder to reach than the Pope. Thankfully, she carved out some time to help Cassidy get ready for her "big night o' love" with Eric.

"Hey, girlie!" she cried, throwing her arms around Cassidy and wrapping her in a hug. "Are you ready to get beautified?"

"Sure." Cassidy grinned. "Just as long as you're not planning any Powerpuff stuff for my eyes."

"Please," Larissa huffed. "That metallic shadow is so last month. I gave mine to the twins next door for dress-up. This summer is all about a light, natural look—paired with a few funky accents, of course."

"Light and natural sounds about right, but hold the funky accents," Cassidy said. "I don't think the punk pixie look is quite right for the occasion."

"Punk pixie!" Larissa squealed. "Oh, Cass, that's brilliant. I wish you were working at Seersucker this summer. You'd be able to add so many good ideas to the fashion show."

"Wow, it took you five whole minutes to mention Seersucker," Cassidy joked. "That's like a record for this summer."

"What do you mean?" Larissa asked, sounding genuinely confused.

Cassidy wondered how to go about telling Larissa that all the fashion talk was getting increasingly annoying, especially because they had such limited time together. "You just talk about it . . . *a lot*."

Larissa frowned. "I'm sorry, it must be hard for you since you can't be there."

Cassidy felt like Larissa had completely missed the point. But it was so nice just having her around that Cassidy decided to drop it. "It's fine, really."

Larissa started digging through her Isabella Fiore paisley hobo bag. "So tonight you're going to finally open your legs and let lover man inside. You nervous?"

"Larissa!" Cassidy protested, her cheeks turning scarlet.

"Come on, it's now or never," she said. "Good thing I brought wax." She reached into her bag and pulled out a small square box of Jolen sensitive skin sugar wax. "You up for a Brazilian? I've become an expert at it."

"No!" Cassidy said, instinctively putting her hands in front of her crotch. "There are some places hot wax just should not go."

"Hey, it's up to you." Larissa shrugged. "But seriously, Cass. Do you think it will happen?"

It was practically all she'd been thinking about, and normally Cassidy would have spilled every fear she had.

But something stopped her just as the words were about to tumble out, and she found herself simply smiling her "I've got a secret" smile instead.

"I knew it!" Larissa squealed. "You and Eric are totally going to do it. Do you have lubricated spermicidal ribbed-for-her-pleasure condoms? I brought a few just in case."

She began rummaging in her bag again, but Cassidy stopped her. "I'm all set, thanks."

"Woo-hoo!" Larissa hooted. "What about your parents? You can use me as a cover story and say you're sleeping over at my house."

"Good, because that's what I already told them."

Larissa grinned. "Cassidy Jones, gettin' freaky at last. So can I interest you in a pedicure at least?"

"That sounds better," Cassidy said. "As long as I get to pick the color."

"You can pick the color if I can pick the music," Larissa offered, already heading for Cassidy's iPod. "Ooh, is this the new Ashanti?"

"Yeah, go for it," Cassidy said as the seductive thump of bass began to fill the room. She glanced at the bottles of nail polish in her makeup drawer and chose a shade called Precious Pearl.

"Is this even a color?" Larissa joked as she filled a baking tin with warm, salty water and began rubbing Cassidy's foot with a pumice stone. "It just looks clear to me."

Cassidy glanced at Larissa's glittering purple toenails. "I thought you said light, natural tones were in this season."

"Well . . . I kind of go for the funky accents."

As they were waiting for the polish to dry, Cassidy was relieved to see that they could fall back into their normal friendship groove. Larissa started talking about all her boy prospects—there was that guy she was hot for at Bar Copa (Cassidy still couldn't picture him or recall his name) and some other FB (short for "foreign babe") named Chico, whom she met at a photo shoot for a Seersucker ad campaign.

Cassidy tried to get up enough courage to tell Larissa about her own boy problems, but she was talking at the speed of light. Did Cassidy knew that even if Larissa would let her talk for more than sixty seconds, she probably wouldn't mention how she was feeling about Zach. Not that Larissa would judge her or anything—her best friend's motto was certainly something akin to "If you can't have sex with the one you love, then do the one you're with." Larissa would probably just say it was a slipup and to forget about it. But that was the thing—she couldn't forget about it *at all*. She thought about Zach a billion times a day, and although she wanted to find a way to express all of this to Larissa, she was unable to. The only thing Cassidy mentioned was how Zach was grading her quizzes and she was doing pretty well so far, to which Larissa replied: "He totally wants you."

Cassidy just ignored the comment and grabbed a *People* magazine that was on the floor near Larissa's bright pink-and-yellow Puma sneakers. But Larissa got Cassidy's attention once she pulled a tube out of her bag and began squeezing green goop into her palm.

Cassidy eyed the goop warily. "What the hell is that?"

"Avocado mask," Larissa said confidently. "To condition and prevent dryness while adding tone and luminosity to the skin."

"You're putting that on my face?"

"Can you think of somewhere better?"

"I don't know, maybe in a salad? I'm not a big fan of this food-in-places-that-aren't-my-stomach stuff."

"Trust me," Larissa urged. "Dina swears by this. If your skin doesn't look amazing, you can beat *her* up." She squeezed the rest of the goop into her palm and tossed the tube in the trash before leaning over Cassidy to pat the green stuff onto her face. Cassidy wrinkled her nose. It smelled like a vegetarian restaurant and felt weird and sticky on her skin.

"So where's he taking you?" Larissa asked.

"No idea. It's all a big surprise. He just told me to be ready for him at eight and to wear something nice."

"Sounds fancy." Larissa put a cucumber slice over each of Cassidy's eyes as her cell phone began to ring. "Hold on, let me get this."

Cassidy swallowed a sigh.

"Fumiko!" Larissa squealed into the receiver. "Oh my God, what's up?" Cassidy could hear her padding into the next room. Was the fashion show really *so* top secret that Larissa couldn't even discuss it with her in the same room?

Cassidy was left with nothing to do but worry about the upcoming evening with Eric. It seemed like a million things could go wrong. What if he guessed what had happened with Zach? She'd been trying to be on her best behavior over the past few weeks, dutifully avoiding Zach and attempting to banish thoughts of him from her mind whenever they appeared, which was like every ten seconds, so it wasn't like she had an easy time of it.

Still, whenever she started to daydream about the kiss in the Hidden Jungle, she would conjure up an image of Eric on his surfboard, his chest rippling in the sunlight. It worked for a little while. Originally she'd thought she could convince herself that all she needed was a steamy night with her boyfriend to forget that Zach even existed. But that theory went kaput within days. Even when she'd felt like she'd cemented Eric's picture firmly in her mind, it seemed like the tiniest thing would remind her of Zach: a chance French word or the smell of an open book.

She was also sketching every day now, and Zach had

become the inspiration for each drawing. She'd made up a bunch of excuses in recent weeks to skip out on plans with Eric just so she could be alone with her pen, paper, and thoughts. She'd returned to the museum where she and Zach first spoke, and sketched a few sculptures. She'd driven all the way to the Aero Theatre in Santa Monica and stood outside for a couple of hours, drawing the 1930s-style marquee. She'd even braved the traffic on the expressway to go to the Los Angeles Zoo and sketch the leopard that she and Zach had encountered in the Hidden Jungle. Actually *being* with Zach seemed like the only thing that could have been better than re-creating all of these things in her notebook. But she'd been avoiding him for so long, she was certain that he wasn't the least bit interested in her anymore.

Cassidy made up her mind right then and there. She needed to tell Larissa everything and get her advice on this. She couldn't hold it inside any longer. Then she would ask Larissa why her face was starting to itch. That was just as disconcerting as what was going on inside her brain.

"Hey, Cass," Larissa called out. Cassidy heard her phone snap shut as she re-entered the bathroom. "Listen, they're having an emergency at the store, and I need to run down there."

"Jesus, Larissa." Cassidy was unable to prevent a whine from creeping into her voice. She reached her hand up to scratch her face, which felt tight and tingly, but brought it down when her fingertips touched the cool goo. "How can you bail on the biggest night of my life?"

"Honey, you'll be just fine." Larissa tried to sound soothing even though Cassidy could tell she was eager to rush off to whatever "emergency" awaited her at Seersucker. "Just keep that mask on for another five minutes. Or is it fifteen? Well, anyway, just take it off when it starts to get hard. And I swear I'll probably be back by then. Wait, maybe not. Anyway, I'll be here in time to help you do your hair. He's coming at eight, right? This should resolve itself in no time once I get there."

Cassidy had never heard Larissa sound so rushed and proud and important and detached all at the same time.

Larissa leaned down to give her a quick pat on the knee, and then she was gone. Cassidy waited until she heard her footsteps disappear down the hall before angrily ripping the cucumber slices from her eyes. Her best friend had just ditched her on what was possibly the most important day of her life. She knew Larissa could be self-absorbed sometimes, but this went beyond that: She felt totally betrayed. Cassidy couldn't tell if her face was itching from the avocado mask or from anger, but she was more than ready to find out. She ran a washcloth under the tap and began scrubbing the avocado off. She didn't stop until every trace of green was gone from her face.

When she finally glanced up at the mirror, a small sob of dismay escaped her lips. She looked like she'd just walked through a beehive. Her face was red and puffy, with pores big enough to drive a truck through.

Cassidy sucked in her breath hard, trying not to let herself cry. She could already feel the tears gathering in her eyes before one broke loose and ran down the scarred landscape of her cheek. Not only was she not looking forward to her big date, now she'd have to go through it looking like a burn victim.

"This can't be fucking happening to me!" she screamed out, knowing no one was around to hear her—not even her mother, who would probably have had a solution to this crisis written down somewhere in her new manuscript: *Timesavers Are Lifesavers—How to Prepare for Unexpected Emergencies and Shave Seconds Off Your Response Time!*

As Cassidy cried, she thought that ever since she'd kissed Zach, nothing had gone right in her life. She almost wished she had never met him. Maybe then she'd still be giggling with her best friend as her skin radiated confidence and health. Maybe she'd brought the bad karma upon herself and was getting exactly what she deserved for doing something so awful to Eric, a totally sweet guy who cared about her a lot.

Or maybe life just sucked.

Cassidy wished there were someone she could turn to, but there was no way she was calling Larissa after what had just happened. The other person she had always confided in was Eric, but she couldn't even imagine how *that* conversation would go. Zach still didn't know she even *had* a boyfriend. If only there were one sane person in the world who she could talk to—just *one*.

Cassidy had never felt so alone in her life. She instinctively reached for her sketchbook, which had always been her solace in times of stress. As she did, the letter she'd written to Joe came fluttering out.

Joe. Of course! Joe was like the only sane person left in the world. She dug out the sheet of notebook paper he'd written his summer contact info on and looked at the phone number at the bottom. He'd said it was for emergencies only—but then again, he'd also said that if she ever really needed to talk, that was enough of an emergency as far as he was concerned.

Her fingers trembled as she pressed the digits into the keypad of her phone, listening to the hollow rings before a female voice answered.

"McCaine Institute."

"Hi." Cassidy tried to steady herself and not sound like an escaped mental patient. "I'm calling for Joe Telesky. This is Cassidy Jones. I really need to talk to him."

"This an emergency?"

"Um, yes," Cassidy said. "It's about . . . his transcript." She had no idea where she'd come up with that, but it seemed to work. If she'd learned one thing over the summer, it was that adults took academics pretty seriously. A few moments later, Joe's breathless, "Hi!" came crackling over the line.

"Cassidy!" he said. "I can't believe you called! How are you? Is everything okay?"

It felt good just to hear his voice. Even with the worry creeping through, he sounded exactly like the fun, reliable Joe she'd known for years. "Yeah, everything's . . ." she was about to say "fine" when she realized how ridiculous that would sound. If everything was fine, why was she calling the emergency line at Camp Crackhead?

"Everything's all screwed up," she said. A sob tripped up through her throat before she could push it back down again.

"What's wrong?"

"It's just . . ." Cassidy struggled to catch her breath. "I'm supposed to go on this big anniversary date with Eric tonight but I kissed Zach and I'm afraid Eric will find out and I think he wants to have sex—Eric, not Zach—and I'm not sure I can, and Larissa was supposed to help me get ready but she flaked to go hang with her stupid fashion people but she left me with this stuff on my face that gave me a rash and now I'm all gross and red and puffy and . . ."

"Whoa," Joe said calmly. "Stop and take a breath,

Cass. That's a lot to process. Let's start with the most immediate thing: your face is red and puffy?"

"Yeah," Cassidy said. "It's really, *really* gross. It's all bumpy and it itches."

"Because you put some avocado stuff on it?" Joe clarified.

"Because a *crazy bitch* put some avocado stuff on it," Cassidy corrected.

Joe chuckled. "At least you can have a sense of humor about it. Now here's what you do: Soak a washcloth in witch hazel, put a bunch of ice in it, and hold it up to your face. Do that for five minutes, then put on some aloe lotion, okay?"

Cassidy headed toward the kitchen for ice. "Are you sure that will work?"

"Positive," Joe said. "We use it around here for poison ivy. It's the same kind of irritation. Do that now while we're on the phone. So you're going out with Eric tonight and you're not really looking forward to it?"

"That's an understatement." Cassidy snorted. She shook several ice cubes out of the tray in the freezer and cradled them in a paper towel. "I mean, I adore Eric and everything, but I'm just not sure this is right anymore."

"Because you kissed Zach?"

"Right," Cassidy admitted reluctantly. "My TA. The one who thinks I should go to art school."

"Isn't he a lot older than you?" Joe asked.

"Well, yeah," Cassidy said. "I mean, he's nineteen. But even though he's older, it feels like we're on the same level. He's just so amazing and I don't know, he just seems to really get me."

"Huh," was all Joe said.

"What?"

"Nothing, it's just . . . older guys sometimes have different priorities, if you know what I mean. I just don't want to see you get hurt. Anyway, what about Eric?"

Cassidy turned on the light in her mother's bathroom and dug around in the medicine cabinet for witch hazel. "I feel awful." She brought the bottle into her bathroom and poured some onto a washcloth. "I mean, how could I *do* that to Eric? I'm such a tramp."

"You are *not* a tramp just because you kissed someone else. Yeah, it's not something you should do all the time, but kissing somebody once doesn't make you a terrible person. You just have to decide what you're going to do about it."

The ice and witch hazel felt cool and soothing on her burning cheeks. "Is death an option?"

She could hear Joe's sharp intake of breath through the receiver. "I don't ever want to hear you say that," he said firmly. "You're smart and funny and cool and beautiful and talented. It would suck indescribably if you weren't around anymore. Besides, I know Camp Crackhead would be a heck of a lot worse without your letters and without my thinking that I'll get to hang out with you when I get home."

"Hey, Joe? I didn't really mean it or anything. I was just . . ." Cassidy sniffled.

"What?" he asked quietly.

"Just . . . thanks," she finally said, sighing.

"Well, I meant it," Joe said firmly. "You've got a friend in Idaho who needs you."

"So what should I do tonight?" Cassidy asked.

"I can't tell you that. Whatever feels right. Maybe you already know what that is. Even if you don't *know* that you know, you're a pretty intuitive person. I'm sure you'll figure it out sooner or later. Just remember, I have faith in you."

"Wow, thanks," Cassidy said. Her tears had stopped, and her breath was beginning to return to normal. Even though she was still confused, at least she didn't feel like jumping out the window anymore. "You really saved my life, Joe."

"Hey, no prob," said Joe.

Cassidy could hear someone in the background calling for him to get off the phone.

"Listen, I have to go," he said. "Good luck tonight, Cassidy."

"Thanks again," she said. "Oh, and Joe?"

"Yes?"

"Don't let the crackheads bite."

She could hear him laughing through the receiver.

"I'll try not to," he said. "Talk to you later."

Cassidy took the washcloth off her face and looked in the mirror. Sure enough, the red bumps were beginning to shrink and fade. She poured some aloe gel into her palm and rubbed it on her cheeks, and the rash slowly disappeared.

Chapter Thirteen

The next thing Cassidy did was go into her bedroom and select the new Gwen Stefani album on her silver iPod mini. If anyone could make her feel better about being a girl, Gwen could. Within an hour, Cassidy was starting to think things might be okay. Her face had returned to normal, and she felt feminine and sexy in a pale pink silk slip dress by Cynthia Rowley with her new, super-sheer Victoria's Secret underwear underneath. She was just brushing her hair so that it fell softly over her bare shoulders when she heard the telltale crunch of gravel in the driveway announcing Eric's arrival.

"Wow," Eric said, sucking in his breath when she came downstairs. "You look amazing."

"You look nice too." She was so used to seeing Eric

in old T-shirts and board shorts that she actually thought he looked a little strange in his light gray suit and maroon silk tie. He'd slicked his hair with gel into tight, gleaming waves, and he smelled like Eternity Summer by Calvin Klein, which her dad wore all the time.

His eyes softened as he leaned down to kiss her, pressing a bouquet of roses into her arms. They were a beautiful deep red, surrounded by white puffs of baby's breath.

"Are you ready?" Eric rubbed his hands together in a quick, nervous gesture that was totally uncharacteristic of his laid-back personality. The energy between them was already stiff and uncomfortable, and they hadn't even left the house.

"I'm ready!" she said, hoping her chipper tone made up for the pangs of worry stabbing through her stomach.

"Great." Eric crooked his elbow and Cassidy took his arm, letting him escort her outside. As the front door closed behind them, she saw a sleek black BMW gleaming on the gravel instead of his usual beat-up Jeep.

"Isn't that your dad's car?" Cassidy asked.

"I wanted to take you out in style." Eric grinned sheepishly. He clicked the key chain so the lights flashed as the doors unlocked. "I'll be mowing the lawn for the rest of the summer for this one."

"Oh, Eric," Cassidy said as he held the passenger door open for her. "You really shouldn't have."

Especially not after what I've done with Zach, she thought.

The car smelled like new leather, and Eric had put on Mariah Carey's *The Emancipation of Mimi* instead of the 50 Cent and Eminem that seemed to follow him everywhere.

"Well, I wanted tonight to be perfect."

Cassidy couldn't think of a single thing to say. She felt terrible that Eric had gone to all this trouble when all she'd been doing lately was cheating and lying and then lying some more. In fact, she was silent the whole time Eric was driving, which amounted to ten long, excruciatingly painful minutes.

"You're quiet even for you," he remarked as they pulled into the parking lot of Geoffrey's, a posh restaurant on the beach. Normally Cassidy would be looking forward to a delicious meal at one of the private tables on the terrace overlooking the ocean, but how was she supposed to eat with a heavy ball of guilt rolling around in her stomach?

"Sorry," Cassidy said. "I guess I'm just . . . a little preoccupied."

"I bet it's that stupid French class," Eric said sympathetically. "They've really been keeping you busy."

"Yeah," Cassidy said. "Busy going on field trips and

putting up with the other nut-jobs in the class." *And don't forget making out with the TA and worrying that you'd find out about it.*

"Well, I've missed you." Eric helped her out of the car like a perfect gentleman. "Life just isn't the same when you're not around every day."

The maitre d' sat them at one of the tables outside. She could hear the clink of glasses and shivers of laughter coming from the other diners, but a white trellis draped in thick, fragrant honeysuckle made it seem like they were all alone. Cassidy breathed deeply as the familiar salt smell of the sea mingled with the flowers. Staring out over the waves, she wished she could run into the ocean and swim away from Eric, the restaurant, and the whole big mess her life had become.

After the waiter came and took their order, there was nothing left to do but talk. Cassidy was really on edge, especially when Eric reached across the table and gently took her hands in his.

"So what's new?" he asked, his eyes gleaming.

Cassidy nervously fiddled with the white napkin that she'd laid on her lap. "Nothing, really."

Jesus, could I be any more obvious?

"How's Larissa?"

"I don't know. We haven't been spending much time together. She's got this insane schedule and I've got class," she explained.

"Sounds like the summer we've been having," Eric commented, his tone suddenly souring.

A bad taste erupted in Cassidy's mouth, so she gulped down a bunch of ice water. "I know I've been kind of unavailable lately. I'm sorry."

He played with his silverware mindlessly. "I didn't get a chance to tell you about the surfing. . . ."

As soon as Eric said "surfing," Cassidy's mind wandered off into the past, where listening to her boyfriend use lingo like "acid drop," "flick off," and "lip turn" made sense to her. There was a time when she hung onto every one of his words, even those she didn't quite understand, but now it was as if she didn't speak his language anymore. In fact, Cassidy was starting to realize that she never did much talking about herself or her interests when she was around Eric. When they'd have a conversation, it'd be centered on him. Actually, when she'd have a conversation with *anyone*, it'd be centered on them.

But that dynamic didn't seem to exist when she'd been with Zach. She felt comfortable expressing herself because he genuinely seemed interested in whatever she had to say.

"Cass? Cassidy?"

She snapped out of her reverie at the sound of Eric's perturbed voice.

"Your phone is ringing."

Cassidy reached down for her bag, which she had stashed underneath her seat. She found her cell beneath her Orbit gum and her Kate Spade wallet right before the caller went to voice mail.

"Hello?"

There was a long pause, then a cough. Finally the person on the other end of the line spoke. "Cassidy, it's Zach."

She gasped so loudly that Eric mouthed the words, "What's the matter?" But she just shook her head, as if to say, "Nothing." It was far from nothing, though. It was an unbelievably gigantic something! Zach had somehow tracked her down, but why?

"I'm sorry to bother you, but I was hoping we could talk," he added. Cassidy just loved how he enunciated each syllable perfectly.

"Yeah, sure. Could you hold on a second?" she said ever so casually.

Eric raised his eyebrows. "Everything okay?"

Cassidy bit her lip. She knew she was about to lie right to Eric's face this time. "Larissa is having some sort of meltdown."

He rolled his eyes. "Figures."

She bolted up from her seat. "I'm going to take this outside. I'll be right back."

Cassidy didn't wait around for Eric to excuse her from the table. She just turned and sprinted out of the restaurant, nearly colliding with a busboy in the process. Cassidy was not about to let anyone get in the way of this phone call.

She darted over to the edge of the parking lot, where Eric's BMW was resting between two Jaguars. She leaned back on the hood of his car and listened to the tide splashing up against the shoreline. It was such a clear night out that Cassidy could see every single star in the sky. She would have stayed out there for hours and drawn a picture of it, but there was something more important for her to do.

Cassidy brought the phone back up to her ear. "Zach, are you still there?"

"Yeah. Where are you?"

"I'm at Geoffrey's, the restaurant near the beach," she said through an anxious hiccup.

Great, now he knows what one of my bodily functions sounds like.

Zach didn't seem to notice. "That's nice," he said. "I hope you don't mind, but I looked through Briand's student log and got your number."

A wide grin swept over Cassidy's face. He went through all that trouble to get in touch with her. That had to be a good sign. "Of course not. What's up?"

"Well, um . . . Wow, this is awkward." Zach sounded very shaky, but Cassidy assumed it was just because of the static. There was no way a sophisticated guy like him would be nervous about talking to *her*, was there? "I just thought maybe we, I mean, you and I could . . . Ever since the zoo, we've kind of lost track of each other and . . . Well, I really want to get to know you more. If that's okay with you and it doesn't weird you out in any way and, Jesus, I need to stop blabbering like an idiot or else you're going to hang up on me and make me really sad."

Cassidy started to giggle. It was refreshing to see Zach acting kind of foolish and vulnerable. It even made him sexier. "I'm not going to hang up."

Zach let out a relieved sigh. "Thank God. I was worried that you hated me or something."

"Why would I hate you?"

"Because you've been, I don't know, sort of distant since our . . . since the jungle," he mumbled. "I assumed that you were upset with me or thought I was some sort of crazy pervert or whatever."

Cassidy laughed again. "No, I've just . . . had a lot on my mind. Really, I'm not mad at you at all."

"Okay, good. I'd really despise myself if you thought I was a lech."

She was so paralyzed with happiness that she couldn't do anything but smile.

"When we can hang out again?" he asked.

"Soon," she said wistfully.

"Like tonight soon or tomorrow soon?"

Cassidy's heart dropped into her stomach when she

remembered what tonight really was—her two-year anniversary with Eric. It was a momentous occasion that could possibly lead to de-virginization. And how was she celebrating? She was trying to make a date with another guy. Except Zach wasn't just "another guy"—he was special. And no matter how remorseful she felt about betraying Eric, she didn't have the willpower within her to say no.

"Tomorrow soon," she replied.

"Sounds great," Zach said, his voice lilting so high that he sounded like a seven-year-old boy. "I'll talk to you later."

"Okay, good-bye," Cassidy said.

She put the phone back in her purse and walked toward Geoffrey's, knowing that she'd have to say good-bye to Eric—tonight soon.

Chapter Fourteen

After dinner, Cassidy and Eric took a virtually silent stroll down the beach to the Casa Malibu Inn. She shivered as a cool breeze swept across the sand, causing the hairs on her arms to stand on end. This was her last chance to tell him the truth and break up with him— or to turn around and run. She begged herself to open her mouth and speak, but before she had a chance, Eric had taken her hand and led her inside.

The lobby was cozy and quaint with sweet-smelling hibiscus flower arrangements. Cassidy could tell Eric was nervous from the way his shoulders hunched when he checked in with the stiffly manicured woman at the front desk. Then he led Cassidy down a long carpeted hallway lined with mirrors to a large elevator that whirred silently up to the master suite. Cassidy felt her heartbeat quicken every time the elevator beeped to indicate that they'd passed another floor. By the time they got to the top, beads of sweat had gathered under her hairline and her hands were clammy and cold. She could feel a different kind of nervous energy emanating from Eric, a kind of excited buzz that seemed to escalate as he shot her a quick, almost embarrassed grin.

Cassidy gasped when Eric opened the door to their room. Lit candles glowed on every surface, illuminating the soft, luxurious draperies and fluffy pillows on the king-size bed. Soft jazz music played in the background, champagne was chilling in a silver stand by the minibar, and a large box of Godiva chocolates sat on the night-stand. A trail of red rose petals led from the door to the bed, and the doors to the balcony were open slightly to let in a soft breeze and the sweet, wild smell of the Pacific. Cassidy remembered all the times she had dreamed of her first night with Eric, a scene just like this. But now she was ten seconds away from regurgitating her grilled salmon dinner and spewing it onto the floor.

"What do you think?" Eric asked eagerly.

"Wow," Cassidy said slowly. "You really went all out."

"Do you like it?" Eric radiated anticipation.

Cassidy wished she could vaporize herself and drift

out the window as a cloud of steam. But Eric's eyes were pleading with her for approval, and she couldn't bear to disappoint him.

"It's beautiful," she said. "I can't believe you did all this."

"It's because you're worth it," Eric said.

He took her in his arms and leaned down for a kiss, opening her mouth with his tongue. He picked her up off the floor and she wrapped her legs around his waist, letting him walk both of them to the bed and set her gently down on the large, soft mattress. He knelt to unbuckle her shoes, kissing her ankles as he undid the straps. She watched him nibble his way up her legs until his head had disappeared under her skirt. She sighed and lay back on the bed. Nothing had felt this good since her kiss with Zach.

Zach! she said to herself. *This should be happening with Zach.* Eric emerged from under her skirt when Cassidy's body suddenly stiffened in his grasp. She knew that if she had sex with Eric right now and her heart was with someone else, she'd regret it for the rest of her life. She had to stop this and now. She was about to pull away when Eric beat her to it.

"Is everything all right?" he asked.

"Yeah . . ." Cassidy had no idea what to say next. "I'm just . . . I don't know. . . ."

"It's okay," Eric whispered. "I know you're nervous. We can take it slow."

He stroked her hair gently and bent to kiss her neck. Cassidy squeezed her eyes shut tight and begged herself to find a way to stop her world from spinning out of control. Eric's mouth was next to her ear, and she could hear his breath growing heavier with excitement. There was no way she could go through with this. Things had already gone too far.

She jerked up so abruptly Eric nearly rolled off the bed. "We need to stop."

"Did I do something wrong?" Eric sat up and smoothed his wrinkled blazer. His forehead creased with worry.

"I just don't think I can do this," Cassidy said miserably. She hugged her knees tightly to her chest. All she wanted to do was make herself as small as possible, so small she could just disappear.

"Why?" Eric asked. Cassidy could tell he was trying hard to be patient and realized how frustrating it must be for him. "I thought tonight . . .Well, I mean, I tried to make everything perfect."

"No," Cassidy whispered. "Everything is beautiful. Dinner was lovely, and this room is so gorgeous, but I just . . . can't."

"I don't understand," he said. "I always thought it was just the wrong time and place. But how can *this* be wrong? We've been together for two years, and we're all alone in a hotel room where nobody can see or hear us."

"I know." Cassidy felt like the most miserable creature in the universe. "It's not that."

"Then what is it? I mean, most people our age who have been together this long are having sex. So why aren't we?"

"Do you really want to know?" Cassidy asked.

"Yes!" Eric nearly shouted. He took a deep breath and ran his hands over his hair. "I mean, yeah. Of course."

"Okay." Cassidy bit her lower lip so hard she nearly drew blood. It was now or never—she had to tell him about her feelings for Zach.

"It's because you never told me you loved me," she found herself saying.

Okay, that's true, but not really the point I should be making right now! Cassidy thought.

Eric's eyes grew huge. "Cass, of *course* I love you! Why would I be with you if I didn't?"

Cassidy didn't answer right away. Her mind was reeling. Her boyfriend had just said the three words she'd been waiting nearly two years to hear, and she found herself wishing desperately that she could make him take them back. Now he would expect her to fulfill *her* part of the bargain—and there was just no way she could go through with it.

"Cassidy," Eric repeated, taking both of her hands in his and looking deep into her eyes. "I love you. I really do."

She could actually feel her heart breaking inside her chest. It felt like pieces of it were crumbling off and splashing into her stomach. "Why didn't you tell me sooner?" she whispered.

"I don't know," Eric said. "It just never occurred to me. I mean, I thought you knew that I loved you. I didn't see why I'd have to say it out loud. Anyway, I can keep saying it. I love you I love you I love you I love you I love you. Do you want me to keep going?"

"No," Cassidy said. She could feel tears gathering in the corners of her eyes. "That's all right. I believe you."

"Good!" Eric said. "So let's start where we left off . . ."

He slid his hand up her knee and under her skirt again, closing his eyes as he leaned in to kiss her neck. Cassidy waited a moment to see if her body would react differently now that she knew beyond a doubt that Eric loved her, but all that happened was that a thick cloud of pain rolled through her. She gently pushed him away once again.

Eric's face twisted with bewilderment. "What now?"

"I'm sorry, Eric," Cassidy said. "I can't."

"Cassidy, why are you doing this to me?" His voice was almost a whine.

"I'm sorry," she repeated.

"I am really, really confused."

"I am too," Cassidy admitted.

She felt the bed shift as Eric stood up. She still couldn't

look at him. "Look, Cassidy, I don't know how to deal with this," Eric said. "Call me when you figure out what you want."

He opened the door and walked out, not even slamming the door behind him. What had she just done? She shivered suddenly in the breeze blowing in through the open terrace doors, wondering if things could possibly have gone worse. She looked guiltily around the room, thinking about all the money and effort Eric had spent trying to make the evening perfect. And she had ruined it. She was the worst girlfriend ever. That is, if she was even Eric's girlfriend anymore. . . .

The tears that were welling up in Cassidy's eyes burned the second she felt a little relieved.

Chapter Fifteen

August 4

Dear Cassidy,

Wow, I don't know what to say. I'm sorry your date went so badly, and I hope you're feeling better now. I wish you had called me, even though it was really late at night and Nurse Ratchet would have read me the riot act. I mean, it was kinda cool getting a letter on stationery from the Casa Malibu Inn, but I still would have preferred a phone call. I hate knowing you were alone there crying all night. And yeah, I know you were crying because of the stains on the paper. Those didn't look like champagne.

So have you spoken to Eric since then? Because from the way you put it in your letter, it kind of sounds like the ball is in your court. If you haven't ended it officially yet, you should probably get around to that soon just so you don't string him along.

I've been thinking about this Zach guy and, I mean, do what you want, but please try not to rush into anything. I know that I shouldn't be handing out relationship advice because, you know, I've never had one. Unless you count the time I dated Therese Craparo in sixth grade for two weeks. I know you thought it was shallow to break up with her because she went by the nickname "Craps," but you'll be happy to know that I haven't had a real girlfriend since, so I got exactly what I deserved—loneliness and a pathetic excuse for a sex life.

So speaking of which, did you know we're not allowed to do it here? Seriously, this guy Dave and this girl Sharlene got caught making out behind one of the outhouses (um . . . gross?) and now they're on "touch bans," which means they're not allowed to go within fifty feet of each other or even make eye contact; otherwise they get twenty extra hours of KP each. You totally think I'm joking, don't you? I'm not. This place is sooo stupid, Cassidy. I mean, of course they're acting like it's this great forbidden love right now, but probably if the counselors just left them alone, they'd be sick of each other in like a week anyway. So retarded.

*I wish I were home in Malibu. Then you could
actually talk to me about what's going on in your life
instead of just writing me letters.*

*Cheers,
Joe*

This wasn't Cassidy's idea of an official first date between her and Zach, but it would have to do. The previous week, she had been in no condition to be sociable, especially because she'd been feeling downright hideous for leading Eric on and screwing with his head. It had practically killed her to cancel on Zach for their "tomorrow soon" rendezvous, but he'd been so sweet and understanding about it. In fact, he'd suggested that they get together the next Friday and Cassidy had jumped at the chance.

However, a few days later Larissa had made her swear on her great-grandmother Eugenia's life to come to see the Seersucker fall fashion extravaganza. Cassidy had thought she'd have to bail on Zach *again*, but luckily he'd agreed to tag along. He'd claimed he absolutely loved haute couture—which Cassidy thought *had* to be a total lie. Zach was as sophisticated as they come, but no self-respecting heterosexual male would be caught dead saying something like that, even if it was a French expression, and Zach happened to be the wise, intelligent (and hotter-than-hot) TA in her French class.

Zach was now driving through the streets of Los Angeles, looking for Smashbox Studios, where the fashion show was being held. Cassidy cranked open her window and let the breeze rush in, ruffling her dark hair as they eased by glitzy storefronts, tall palm trees, and the gorgeous, flawless people who were strolling the streets at dusk. She glanced at Zach and thought about how he belonged on the runway himself. Sure, he was a little short, but everything else about him was ethereal and sublime. His jaw was very angular and his eyes seemed so wide all the time, like he was absorbing everything he encountered and filing it all away in his memory. Cassidy even thought his ears were delectable—especially the little extra flap of skin up at the top of his right one. This tiny, insignificant physical flaw just made him even more distinctive and unique.

And he was mere inches away from her. All Cassidy had to do was lean over and lick him from head to toe, but then that could cause a major traffic accident and the cops would get called and everyone in Malibu would know that she was involved with her TA.

If you call one earth-shattering kiss "involved," she thought.

"Are you excited about the show?" Zach asked, taking his eyes off the road for a second and delivering a "stop dead in your tracks and gawk at me" smile.

Cassidy's face was completely void of enthusiasm. "Can't you see how thrilled I am?"

Zach chuckled. "Remember that thing I said about liking haute couture?"

She nodded.

"Big fat lie."

"I thought so," she said knowingly.

"My ex-girlfriend forced me to go to all these fashion galas in New York and I absolutely hated it," he explained. "But I'm making an exception, just for you."

Cassidy felt conflicted. She was so thrilled that he'd complimented her, but it was only *after* he'd brought up his ex. She had to get to the bottom of it. "Did you guys, like, live together or anything?"

Zach smirked. "It wasn't that serious."

She was so relieved that her pulse returned to its normal rate. But when she reminded herself that she currently had a boyfriend, whom she hadn't had the courage to "ex" yet, her stomach churned to the point where she might have to barf in her Bric's white nylon tote bag.

"Besides, it's easier for starving writers like me to hone their craft when they don't have to pay rent. That's why I trained to be an RA—free housing is definitely worth babysitting a bunch of hyper freshmen."

"If you're not into freshmen, what are you doing hanging out with someone still in high school?" she asked.

"Who, you?" Zach playfully shoved her with his

shoulder. "You're extraordinary, Cassidy. Half the time, I forget that you're not in college."

Cassidy felt her cheeks glow as Zach's gray Nissan Xterra pulled into the valet parking lot of Smashbox Studios. Zach got out and handed the attendant his keys, then walked around and helped Cassidy out of the car. When she placed her clammy, sweaty hand in his, she felt a jolt of energy rush to every neuron in her system. Her attraction to Zach went that deep.

They followed the signs for the fashion show down a long, dim hallway. The throbbing music that had been nothing but a hint of muddy bass when they entered grew stronger until the hallway took a sharp turn and they suddenly found themselves in a dazzling auditorium packed with people. Light projections flitted across the white curtains that hung at one end of the room, and a runway jutted into the crowd.

"How are we supposed to find Larissa in here?" Cassidy asked, eyeing the solid wall of impeccably dressed audience members laughing and mingling around her.

"Perimeter check," Zach said. "Let's walk around the outside of the room and see if we can spot her."

He held out his hand and Cassidy took it again, feeling the warmth seep into her palm as Zach snaked expertly through the clumps of people lingering on the fringe of the crowd. Everyone seemed glossy and slightly pretentious, wearing haughty scowls and "look at me" accessories. Cassidy had tried to put some flair into her outfit for the occasion, adding a flowing yellow scarf belt and some dangly earrings to her tan miniskirt and black tank top ensemble, but looking around, she felt like she'd been born and raised in the Gap. If it wasn't for Zach, who was still clutching her hand and leading the way, she'd feel so out of place.

"There she is," Zach said suddenly.

Cassidy looked up from the sea of fur-trimmed boots and snakeskin stilettos she'd been staring down at and caught a glimpse of Larissa standing in a tight clump with Fumiko, Dina, and Toby—the guy Larissa had been raving about the last time they all went out dancing. Together they made a beeline for the group, but Cassidy had to remember to slip her hand out of Zach's at the last minute.

"Cassidy! Zach!" Fumiko cried. She leapt out of the circle and gave them hugs as they approached. Her cheeks were pink with excitement. "Glad you guys could make it."

"So am I," Cassidy said. "I know you've all been putting a ton of time into this. There's no way I'd miss it."

"Yeah, really. We've been pulling all-nighters for the past week to get all the sewing done," Larissa said with practiced exhaustion. Cassidy couldn't tell if she actually looked tired from staying up late sewing or from the rings of smoky shadow she'd layered around her eyes to create a very professional-looking cracked-out heroin-chic look.

"I'm sure it will be worth it," Cassidy assured her. "I can't wait to see what you came up with."

Toby ran his hand over his shaved head. "I'm going to get a beer. Anyone want?"

Everyone except Cassidy raised their hands. Toby looked at her questioningly.

"I'm Amish," she joked.

Cassidy was beyond pleased that Zach was the only one who laughed.

"I'll be back in five," Toby said.

"I'll go with you!" Larissa volunteered quickly. "You're going to need some help carrying all those beers."

She noticed how Larissa's earlobes had turned red, which only happened when she was embarrassed. Cassidy's interest was definitely piqued—maybe some-thing was going on between her and Toby. She and Larissa had been on acquaintance-level speaking terms since the Avocado Incident, so she was way, *way* out of the loop.

But before she could whisk Larissa away to the bath-room for a quick catch-up session, Toby sauntered away and her best friend scampered after him in her distressed leather Steve Madden boots with three-inch heels.

"So have you really been pulling all-nighters for the past week to get this finished on time?" Zach asked. "You must be ready to drop."

Dina laughed. "Actually, it was just some late nights the past couple of days," she said. "I think Larissa was exaggerating a little."

"She's been known to do that," Cassidy said. "It seems like she's been really busy helping you guys, though."

"Oh, don't get me wrong, she's been a huge help," Dina said. "But you know, we kind of have the whole thing under control. I mean, we *did* go to school for this. Mostly we've all just been hanging out."

Cassidy felt blood throb through her temples. It hurt enough when Larissa made it seem like she was ditching her to solve the fashion crisis of the twenty-first century, but ditching her just to hang out? That was total bullshit. She took a deep breath and felt Zach's hand discreetly reach over to pat her on the small of her back. A wave of calm rolled over her at his touch.

"What have you been up to this summer?" Fumiko asked Cassidy and Zach, slipping her thumbs through the belt loops of her vintage-wash Joie jeans. "Keeping busy with French class?"

"Yeah, we had another field trip the other night," Cassidy said. "We went to see *Vivre sa vie*. Have you heard of it?"

"Omigosh, I *love* Godard!" Fumiko squealed. "His films are so stylish. I always wanted to do my eye makeup like his heroines'."

"Funny, I actually tried the other day," Cassidy said, laughing at the memory. "But I ended up looking more like Courtney Love on a bender than Anna Karina on the silver screen."

The entire group burst into laughter, and it took a moment for Cassidy to register that they were laughing at what she had said. She had never been able to make an entire group of people laugh. Sure, she'd just made Zach giggle a minute ago, which she thought was progress. But this type of response was really unusual. On the few occasions when she had gotten over her shyness enough to say anything at all, people looked at her like she was a lost child asking strangers in the grocery store whether they'd seen her mommy.

This is so strange, she thought. *Being the center of attention feels kind of . . . good.*

"What's so funny?" Larissa asked as she and Toby returned with the beers. Her cheeks were flushed and her forehead wrinkled into a tiny frown.

"Oh, Cassidy was just telling us about a makeup mishap she had," Dina explained. She stuck a thumb in the neck of her Corona and flipped it over so a spray of white fizz engulfed the lime. "Don't you hate it when those happen?"

"They don't really happen to me," Larissa said in a breezy tone. "I know what I'm doing when it comes to makeup."

"Like the time you put an avocado mask on my face and I broke out in hives?" Cassidy couldn't help reminding her.

"Wow, did that really happen?" Dina asked. "That sucks."

"It wasn't exactly a shining moment," Cassidy said. "I looked like someone had lopped off my head and replaced it with a sun-dried tomato."

To her surprise, everyone laughed at the gross image she'd painted. It was like suddenly she was Chris Rock or something. Then Cassidy noticed the only one who wasn't enjoying her sense of humor was Larissa.

"Is this that avocado mask I'm into?" Dina asked Larissa. "Because you know you're supposed to do a test patch twenty-four hours in advance, right? Some people really *are* allergic."

"Guess I learned that the hard way," Larissa mumbled. She looked so miserable that Cassidy decided to change the subject—even though she had to admit to herself that it felt just a tiny bit good watching Larissa squirm.

"So Toby," Cassidy said, "Larissa told me you're a graffiti artist. That's so cool. What kind of stuff do you do?"

Toby grinned. "I'd need a wall to show you," he said.

"But here's a small example." He rolled up his sleeve to reveal the word *Fresh* tattooed in bright, intricate letters on his forearm.

"Wow, that's amazing," Cassidy said, genuinely impressed. "You designed that?"

"Yeah." Toby grinned almost shyly. "And my friend Ryan inked it. It's based on a tag I did on a warehouse up in Oakland."

"Sweet," Zach said, rolling up his own sleeve. "Check mine out."

Toby eyed Zach's tattoo and nodded approvingly. "Your design?" he asked.

"No, my friend's," Zach said. Then he told the story about taking the dare in Paris. He finished to peals of laughter from the group just as the lights began to dim and the music swelled from a low, wavering hum into a loud, rhythmic beat. Suddenly all the lights went up and the runway exploded with tall, leggy models wearing string bikinis and long feathered capes.

Cassidy found herself clapping and catcalling along with the crowd. Her mind was still reeling from the conversation she'd just had. For once in her life, she'd actually been able to talk to a group of people without feeling completely out of place and tongue-tied. It wasn't even that big a deal—all she had to do was open her mouth and be herself. Had her newfound confidence come from having Zach along, or was she just getting used to talking to people on her own?

As the models began strutting back and forth in fashionable fall tweeds, Cassidy glanced at Larissa, who had her arms crossed in front of her chest and a pout on her face that could rival any bratty five-year-old's.

"Oh, here comes ours!" Fumiko exclaimed as the lights dimmed to a shimmering violet and the speakers boomed out a sultry down-tempo beat.

The first model emerged, wearing a bright patchwork skirt with a crocheted top and soft leather sandals.

"She looks amazing," Fumiko squealed, clutching Dina's arm. "That necklace was a perfect touch."

As the models strolled across the runway, posing and turning, Fumiko and Dina dissected each of their outfits in excruciating detail, commenting on everything from their eye shadow to the stitching on their shoes. Even Larissa was dropping her cooler-than-thou act.

"I did most of the work on this one," she whispered to Cassidy, pointing at a flowing turquoise dress splashed with silver flowers.

"It's gorgeous," Cassidy assured her, feeling genuinely proud. Maybe Larissa really *did* have a future as a designer after all.

"Did you remember to take up the hem?" Dina whispered to Larissa just as the model reached the lip of the runway and stopped to pose and turn. Larissa's face went white. A moment later, the sound of silk tearing screeched across the room as the model stepped on the end of the extra-long skirt, ripping the dress with the force of her body spinning toward the rear of the stage.

An audible gasp rang out through the warehouse and a quick look of panic flashed across the model's face as she realized her thong was visible to hundreds of people. But she quickly regained her composure, scooped up the ruined fabric, and wrapped it around her as she strutted regally toward the exit.

Larissa's lower lip was trembling.

"Sweetie, it's okay," Dina said, reaching out to pat her shoulder. "We all make mistakes. No big deal."

But Larissa just turned and stumbled toward the back of the room, running awkwardly on her heels like a baby giraffe taking its first steps. Silence seemed to hang over the group despite the loud music pounding in the background.

"I'll go find her," Cassidy volunteered. Zach gave her hand a quick squeeze before she turned to burrow through the crowd. She spotted Larissa by the bar, downing a gin and tonic and shakily unwrapping a Twizzler.

"It's okay, Larissa," Cassidy said. "This could have happened to anyone."

"Yeah, sure, whatever," Larissa said, her voice quaking. "It's okay as long as you don't care that my future as a designer just went down the drain."

"It didn't!" Cassidy argued. "It's not the end of the world, seriously. I don't think most people even noticed."

Larissa barked out a short, sarcastic laugh. "Thanks for the sentiment, but you'd have to be blind not to notice that."

"Well, Fumiko and Dina said it was fine," Cassidy tried again, wishing Larissa would at least meet her eyes. "They aren't mad or anything."

"Yeah, I guess you'd know that, since you're all tight with them now," Larissa said coldly. She bit angrily into the Twizzler.

"What do you mean?" Cassidy asked.

"Nothing. Whatever."

"No, really . . . what are you talking about?"

"Just that you're suddenly all chatty around them," Larissa said reluctantly. She tried to shrug it off with a laugh. "I mean, what's up with that?"

Cassidy reminded herself that Larissa was just upset about the mishap. She struggled to swallow the bubble of anger rising in her throat.

"I was just talking to them," she said. "You know, polite conversation?"

Larissa's lips set in a hard line across her face. "Well, from where I was standing, it looked like you were try-ing to impress them."

"No, I wasn't," Cassidy protested. "We were just chatting. I *am* allowed to talk to your friends, aren't I?"

"Well, sure," Larissa said. "But I mean, you don't have to try so hard. It comes off looking really uncool."

The bubble of anger burst in Cassidy's throat. "First of all," she spat, "I was *not* trying to impress them. Second of all, who else am I supposed to talk to with you ignoring me all the time?"

"I'm talking to you right now, aren't I?" Larissa rummaged in her bag for another Twizzler and avoided Cassidy's sharp gaze.

"Only because I followed you over here. You've barely called me once in the last month."

"I've been busy with this show."

"So I heard," Cassidy said acidly.

"And what's *that* supposed to mean?"

"Dina told me you haven't been pulling all-nighters. She said you've mostly just been hanging out. You could have at least called me." Cassidy had to struggle to get the words out. She didn't *want* to be arguing with Larissa—she wanted to be comforting her. But it was hard with Larissa being so mean and aloof at the same time. Cassidy felt like she was talking to a catty stranger instead of her best friend. "It's just that . . . I would have liked to have spent some time with you this summer," she said quietly.

"It's not *my* fault you're stuck in French class all day," Larissa said.

"That's not the point!" Cassidy said, anger and frustration throbbing in her temples. "It's not like I've ceased to exist just because we aren't working at Seersucker together."

Larissa's nostrils flared the way they always did when she got mad. "Well, I am working there, and I care about my reputation, so I'd appreciate it if you could just go back to being quiet and stop embarrassing me."

Cassidy was so stunned it took her a moment to find her voice. "So that's what this is about. You're upset because I actually have the guts to talk to people now. You're afraid I'm going to steal your spotlight or something."

Larissa snorted. "Hon, you're being ridiculous. I'm just afraid you're going to make an ass of yourself in front of my friends and then *I'll* look bad."

Cassidy stared openmouthed at the girl who she had trusted more than anyone. "I can't even believe you just said that. I've never seen you like this before."

"I'm just being honest," Larissa said matter-of-factly. "And if you can't deal with it, tough. You need to grow up, Cassidy."

"I *am* grown up!" Cassidy nearly shrieked. She lowered her voice, realizing that the people around them were starting to stare. "You just haven't been around to notice it."

Larissa rolled her eyes and sighed. "Listen, I didn't mean what I said, okay? I'm just . . . Ugh, I'm missing the show! Can we talk about this later?"

Cassidy had done something she'd never done before—she'd argued with Larissa. Actually, it was the first real argument that she'd had with anyone. It was a major step in the Cassidy-growing-up process. She'd spoken her mind without being self-conscious or worrying about how the other person was going to respond. Even though she was mad at Larissa right now, she was also kind of proud of herself.

Which was why she felt very confident when she very tersely said, "Oh, I am *so* done talking to you."

However, Larissa didn't seem too proud of Cassidy or happy about her new ability to speak her mind. Larissa spun on her heel so fast the wedge of lime flew off the rim of her cup and landed on the floor, where it was immediately squashed under somebody's blue fur boot.

Cassidy felt the room spinning around her, her heartbeat echoing in her ears. She took a deep breath and then another, wondering why they both came out ragged. When she reached up to rub her eyes, which suddenly felt full and itchy, her finger came back wet. She hadn't even realized she was crying until Zach showed up and put both of his arms around her.

Chapter Sixteen

Even though she'd spent a lot of time hanging out on the Pepperdine campus with Zach after class, everything looked different at night. After they'd left Smashbox Studios, he'd insisted on taking Cassidy out for a while to get her mind off the infamous Jones versus King bitch-fest. It had seemed like a great idea, especially because when Cassidy had checked her phone in the car, she noticed her inbox was filled with text messages from Eric.

WHERE R U?
CAN WE TALK?
I MISS U

When Cassidy had tossed her phone in her bag and buried her head in her hands, she'd wanted nothing more than to run for cover. Lo and behold, Zach had perceived her feelings without her having to speak them. At the same time, she'd felt like she could say just about anything to him, including those three words she'd wanted Eric to utter so desperately.

"This way." Zach was leading her down one of the winding paths that were illuminated gently with dim, old-fashioned streetlamps.

"Where are we going?" Cassidy asked.

"You'll see," he said mysteriously. "Somewhere I know you like."

The path wandered into a shadowy grove overhung with trees.

"I can't see a thing out here," Cassidy said, reaching out her hand to feel ahead of her in the blackness. She touched something warm and soft—Zach. She felt his fingers slipping around hers and held his hand tightly until they emerged into a clearing.

"It's the duck pond!" Cassidy gasped, bursting into relieved laughter. "We were just here this afternoon."

"Isn't it even prettier when the lights are bouncing off it?" Zach asked quietly.

Cassidy had to agree. The pond's ripples reflected the streetlamps so that they shimmered like thin gold necklaces on the water's surface. Aside from the occasional swan gliding by or student biking down one of the nearby paths, the night was silent. Cassidy's worries were so far from her mind, and the only thing that seemed to exist in the world was the person next to her.

Zach took a seat next to Cassidy on a park bench. She savored the closeness and silence so much that she wished she could get out her sketchbook and draw it. Then Cassidy remembered that she'd stashed it in her tote bag earlier that morning. She looked at the way Zach's brow was glowing in the iridescent moonlight and his flawlessly shaped lips, which were this amazing shade of ruby red. She couldn't help herself any longer.

"Zach," she whispered. "Would you mind if I–" Her words were catching in her throat.

He took her hand and brushed a stray hair that had been stuck to Cassidy's cheek. "What is it?"

Cassidy steadied herself and took a deep breath. "Do you think I could sketch you right now?"

Zach flashed her a brilliant smile. "I'd be honored."

Within seconds, she yanked out her notebook and pencil and stared at Zach intensely. Cassidy grinned when she realized that she didn't have to even study Zach in order to re-create his portrait. She'd been gawking at him for so long, she had every single one of his features memorized. After a few minutes of drawing the outlines of his face and then shading it in with lots of detail, Cassidy presented him with her work of art.

Zach took the notebook in his hands and chuckled, which caught Cassidy off guard. Did he think it was bad? This was the first time she'd ever drawn a picture of someone that wasn't a cartoon, and the thought of him not liking it was killing her.

Actually, it was the thought of him not liking *her*.

"This is fantastic," he said with another giggle.

"Then why are you laughing?" she asked, squirming.

Zach cleared his throat and pasted a serious expression on his face. "I'm not laughing. It's just that . . . I look much better in this sketch than I've ever looked in my entire life."

Cassidy was ecstatic. "So you like it?"

"I told you, it's fantastic. That's why I'm not giving it back."

"Maybe I want to keep it for myself," she blurted.

Oh, God, why did I just say that?

"You don't need this, though. I'm right here."

Cassidy turned her gaze downward for a moment and thought about that day in the Hidden Jungle. Although it happened weeks ago, her attraction to Zach had only gotten stronger. All the guilt she had been feeling about Eric was nowhere to be found now, and any sadness she had been experiencing over Larissa seemed to be locked in suspended animation.

She and Zach were truly alone, and she couldn't have been happier.

Or more ready.

Cassidy looked up at him and realized he'd been staring at her, his eyes brewing with intensity. Their lips met softly in the darkness, her heart tripping through her chest, her hands on his shoulders, touching him in ways she'd been dying to touch him ever since they'd met. She closed her eyes as he nibbled gently at her neck, kissing her earlobes. She heard herself moan quietly.

"We should stop," Zach gasped. He pulled back a little bit but kept his hands around her waist.

"I don't want to," she said, drawing him in again. The stubble on his cheeks was like fine grains of sand under her lips. She grasped at him so that they both tumbled onto the ground, rolling around in the dewy grass.

"You're beautiful, Cassidy. I want you so much," Zach breathed into her ear. The full length of his body was against her and then on top of her.

"Maybe we should go to your dorm?" she whispered, moving against him instinctively, too turned on to stop.

"Are you sure you want to do that?" he asked.

"Yes," she said firmly.

She had never been more sure of anything in her life.

*　　*　　*

Looking back, what Cassidy remembered most wasn't the

big moment, but the details: how the bright light from the small desk lamp in Zach's dorm room had startled them both so much he had to throw his T-shirt over it; the way she'd been surprised at first to see that his chest was as smooth and hairless as a young boy's; the moment when he couldn't untie the yellow scarf around her waist and his forehead started to wrinkle with frustration but when he met her eyes, they both dissolved in laughter.

What she remembered afterward was the way she buried her nose in his neck and let his smell surround them like a cloud, settling over her skin until it felt like it was her smell too. Even though she was sticky and sweaty when it was over, her first thought was that she never wanted to shower again—that if she had things her way, she would smell like Zach for the rest of her life. And when they were done, she lay back on the pillow feeling almost numb with fatigue but at the same time more alive than she'd ever felt before. Zach propped his head on his hand, elbow on the bed next to her. With his other hand he traced delicate figures on her skin.

Dawn crept in through the window, turning the light in the room a cool, quiet gray. Neither of them spoke. Cassidy had never felt so close to anyone. Zach's eyes, usually so green they were nearly blinding, had mellowed to reflect the morning light. She had never seen him look so peaceful and content, Cassidy thought before falling into a deep, dreamless sleep with Zach's body warm and solid beside her.

Chapter Seventeen

August 11

Dear Joe,

Congratulations! Now that Larissa and I aren't speaking, I think you've officially taken her place as my best friend. Too bad you're so far away—I wish I had a best friend I could actually talk to.

Guess what? I'm not a virgin anymore, and it feels so weird. The worst part is I think you may have been right about rushing into things. After Zach and I first kissed, I avoided him for a while and now the same thing is happening, but worse. He's been very aloof toward me. All this week, he hasn't stuck around to talk to me after class like he usually does. I mean, I guess he can't let on that something's up with us *because if anyone at Pepperdine found out, he'd be in so much trouble. But still, I feel like I've been socked in the gut. It gets worse. Eric was waiting for me in the school parking lot this morning. And I didn't even have the nerve to break up with him right then—I said we'd meet up tomorrow. I'm such a jackass! So now:*

(a) I have to dump Eric tomorrow and I totally feel like this awful person who cheated on her nice boyfriend who was great to her for two years. It's like being some soap opera villain and I'm so not used to feeling like the bad guy.

(b) I don't know what's going on with Zach.

(c) I'm not speaking to my best friend.

Argh! Sorry I'm such a mess. I wish I had something cute or funny to tell you, the way you always have something cute or funny to tell me, even when it seems like your life totally sucks. Maybe next time.

> *Unhappily yours,*
> *Cassidy*

The sun was just beginning to set over the Pacific as Cassidy pulled into the parking lot near Point Dume. She sat in her car for a moment, thinking she could still turn back. She imagined driving away from the beach and Eric, away from Larissa and Malibu and the giant weird mess her life had become. She could drive down to Mexico, get a job picking guavas, and live in a hut on the beach, wear flowers in her hair, and never have to deal with breaking up with anyone ever again.

Yeah. Who was she kidding? She was sixteen, and her passport was locked away in a safe-deposit box in the vault of her parents' bank—after all, her mother's first self-help book was titled *Mind Over Money: Think Your Way to a Nest Egg That Matters*. Besides, she *hated* guavas.

Cassidy stepped onto the beach, slipping off her shoes to let the cool sand ease between her toes. She thought as she stared out over the ocean that there was no way she could actually do this without throwing up, passing out, or possibly just dropping dead. Heading toward the water, she cupped her hand over her eyes to deflect the glare and gazed out to sea. There were three bodies still paddling their surfboards out toward the waves, but none of them was Eric.

Maybe I could just go and wade in a little bit before I have to do this, Cassidy thought. She realized she was procrastinating and turned and headed toward the faded driftwood shack where the employees of Carl's Surf Shack kept their boards. The door was slightly ajar, and as she pushed it open, she had to wait a moment for her eyes to adjust to the dim light. Sunshine filtered through the cracks in the walls, making wavy patterns on the floor that made her feel like everything was underwater.

Boards and wetsuits hung from the pegs on the wall and the shack smelled of surf wax, rubber, and salt.

Eric's board rested between two sawhorses and he was leaning over it, waxing the edges with a soft green chamois. He looked up when she came in and Cassidy had to suppress a gasp—he looked different than he had just a couple of short weeks ago on their anniversary. His face seemed more drawn, his posture droopier. Still, his lips parted in a huge smile when he saw her, and a bit of the usual sparkle returned to his eyes. He was wearing board shorts and a Hawaiian shirt open to reveal his hard, gleaming chest. He had a better body than Zach, Cassidy realized. But that didn't seem to matter in the least right now.

"Cassidy," he said. "I was worried you weren't going to come."

"So was I," she said. They both laughed nervously. The air in the shack suddenly felt unbearably moist.

"Eric, I . . ." Cassidy began, but she couldn't finish. She'd practiced what she had to say over and over again in her head on the drive over, but suddenly her mind was a huge, fuzzy blank.

Eric came out from around the surfboard. "Cassidy, I'm so sorry about how things went on our anniversary. I shouldn't have left you all alone like that."

The fuzz in her head thickened. Why was *Eric* apologizing? *She* was the one who had slept with someone else! For a minute, Cassidy thought how easy it would be to just accept his apology and pretend nothing had ever happened with Zach. She and Eric could stay together, finish up high school as the couple they'd been for the last two years. She could forget that Zach even existed. Everyone was allowed to slip up once, right? But that train of thought fizzled out as quickly as a Fourth of July sparkler.

Spit it out already! she commanded herself sternly.

"Eric, we've had such great times together and you've been really good to me, but . . ."

"But what?" Eric's eyes were watering at the corners.

The words came tumbling out of her mouth in a rush, not making sense. She felt like she was tripping over her own tongue.

"I think you're a great person and you're very kind and attractive and a good surfboarder and I probably don't even deserve you and maybe we can still be friends, I mean I really hope we can because I think you're so great and nice and everything and–"

"Cassidy," Eric interrupted, struggling to keep his voice calm. "Are you breaking up with me?"

"Yes." It was the most difficult syllable she'd ever uttered. She could barely choke out the rest. "I am."

There. She'd said it. And it felt . . . *awful.* Like running over your grandmother with a truck, then putting the truck in reverse and backing over her to make sure she was dead. Eric appeared so hurt and stunned that she wished she could suck the words back into her mouth like soda through a straw.

"Why?" Eric asked. His broad, strong shoulders were trembling.

"I don't know," she said quietly. "I mean, it's really not you. Really. Not at all. I mean, I guess it's me. I've changed a lot this summer, and sometimes I feel like I don't even really know who I am anymore."

"Is there someone else?"

"Yes," Cassidy whispered. Silence came crashing down between them like the curtain at the end of a play's second act. She could hear waves rolling in the distance and Eric's ragged breathing.

"Who?" he finally asked.

"You don't know him," she said. At least she could be honest about that. Not that it made her feel any better.

"I can't believe this," he murmured.

"I can't either." Cassidy struggled to hold back tears. "I never, ever wanted to hurt you this much. I feel so terrible." Her voice broke and she let it, let Eric see the tears leak out down her cheeks and her chest shiver.

"This just wasn't supposed to happen," Eric said quietly.

Cassidy crossed her arms in front of her chest to keep her heart from jolting out. At the end of the school year, she'd thought she was in love with Eric and was convinced they were happy. Now she didn't even know what she wanted—and she'd hurt someone she cared about in the process. "Listen, you don't have to forgive me right away," she said through her tears. "You don't have to forgive me ever. I don't blame you if you hate me for the rest of your life because I'll totally deserve it. But I do want you to know that I care about you, and I'm sorry I hurt you, and I'll always think of you as a wonderful person and a great friend."

Her eyes were so blurry with tears she could barely make her way out the door of the shack. As soon as she was outside, she collapsed on the sand, curling into a ball and sobbing with her fist stuck in her mouth to prevent her wails from traveling to the few twilight surfers still straggling up the beach. Sand crept into her nostrils and embedded itself in her hair, but she didn't care. All she could think of was what an awful thing she had done.

She felt a large, warm hand on her shoulder and looked through the veil of hair that had fallen over her face to see Eric crouching over her. His chin was trembling.

"Cassidy, listen," he said.

She sat up and brushed a layer of hair and tears out of her eyes. Eric sat down next to her on the sand and took a deep breath.

"I am really, really mad at you," he began.

"You should be," she interrupted. "I'm mad at me too."

"But I can tell you feel bad," Eric continued. "I think

maybe I kind of knew something was going on. I mean, you've never been very good at hiding things." He took a deep, shaky breath. "So I can't say that I'll forgive you right away. That's going to take a long time. But . . . well, maybe I'll be able to someday. And I guess that's going to have to do for now."

"Thanks." Cassidy sniffled. "That's more than I expected. I really appreciate it."

Some seagulls swooped onto an abandoned sand-wich several feet away, cackling gleefully as their long shadows stretched across the sand.

"You know," Eric said after a while, "I want you to be happy."

Cassidy looked over at him, surprised. His shoulders were squared against the setting sun and he had almost managed to twist his mouth into a smile.

"I want that for you too," she replied.

They sat in silence together until the beach was dark and the hairs on their arms stood up in the cool breeze. Then he walked her to the Volvo, they hugged briefly, and drove off in separate directions into the night.

Chapter Eighteen

August 18

Dear Cassidy,

I'm really sorry to hear about Eric. Breaking up sucks—not that I've had much experience with it. But you can take comfort in the fact that I watched *The OC* once, so I know it's really tough. I think you did the right thing, though, as hard as it was. You shouldn't pursue something your heart isn't in, and I guess your heart wasn't really in it with Eric anymore.

I hate to say I told you so about Zach because obviously you're really hurt. If it's any consolation to you, I'm almost never right about anything, and if I were there, I'd definitely beat him up now that I'm all strong *from lugging a sixty-pound backpack through the wilderness and doing eighty billion hours of KP. I'd protect your honor, throw down the gauntlet, ALL that. But I can't, so all I can do is tell you I hope things get better soon.*

I'm sorry I didn't respond to your letter sooner, but we had to do these solo wilderness trips to "focus our minds on our personal growth" or something. I thought it was going to suck being out in the woods all by myself for three days, but right before I left, one of the counselors slipped me this book called The Meaning of Mindfulness. *It's by this Tibetan monk and it's all about being aware of everything that's around you, even the tiny little things, and learning to enjoy them. I know it sounds dumb, but reading this book, combined with being all alone on top of this mountain with 360-degree views of all these beautiful pine forests—suddenly I was like WHOA, my eyes opened up, and now I actually SEE all the beauty around me that I was missing before. It makes everything easier: dealing with the other kids here, missing my bed and all my friends and you—it's like I can handle it now.*

I wish you were here to see how beautiful the Idaho mountains are and feel what it's like to swim in a freezing cold lake at sunrise. I wish I could

*send you a little bit of all the nature here to make
you feel better.*

> *Love,*
> *Joe*
>
> *P.S. Eat some cookie dough for me.*

Something's gotta give, Cassidy thought as she rounded the corner at the foot of her street, watching the pavement streak by under her sneakers. Beads of sweat began to pop out on her forehead, and she felt one trickle down her back under her sports bra.

It was the first time in over a year that she had gone running for any reason other than to not fail gym. But after several days of nothing but French class and drawing for her art school portfolio, she just had to get out of the house and actually *do* something.

Something's gotta give, she thought again as she huffed up a hill lined with McMansions, the sweat beginning to drip down her face. After all, things couldn't get much worse. She'd dumped her boyfriend, her best friend wasn't speaking to her, and Zach was acting like he'd forgotten she existed.

She still couldn't figure out if he'd just used her for sex, and it hurt to even think about it. But as she sank into the rhythm of her sneakers hitting the pavement, she realized she had to find out. Zach would be leaving for New York and college in a couple of weeks, and she refused to let him go forever without knowing why he shared such an intimate moment with her if he was hell-bent on pushing her away. You only lost your virginity once, and she wasn't going to let the guy she'd done it with just drift off into the netherworld without knowing for sure what had been going on.

Maybe Zach wasn't exactly ready to drop everything to stay with her forever—she still couldn't totally believe that he'd just stopped being into her after they had sex. Something in his eyes on those rare occasions when she managed to catch his gaze in French class made her think that Zach still cared about her. A lot.

So what was she going to do about it? The old Cassidy Jones would have just waited for Zach to say something, but not the new-and-improved, assertive, proactive Cassidy she was starting to become. *That* Cassidy would take initiative. She'd have to make a plan. As she started up the next hill and her lungs opened up to take in the sticky California air, that's exactly what she did.

*   *   *

"Zach!" Madame Briand had just dismissed the class, and Cassidy literally had to run after him and grab his arm in the hallway to get him to stop walking.

"Oh, hey, Cass," he said, trying to sound casual, as if he hadn't slept with her and then ignored her for two weeks. "What's up?"

"Listen, I desperately need your help with something," she said.

"Yeah?" Zach looked cagily around the hallway, which was full of students straggling out of class. "Okay, fine. Let's talk." He walked so quickly to a discreet nook near the water fountain that Cassidy practically tripped over her feet trying to keep up with him. She had to slow down and remind herself that her plan did *not* involve falling to the floor and breaking her nose.

"So, what's going on?" Zach leaned against the wall and looked down at her in that special way that still made her heart flutter. "What do you *desperately* need my help with?"

Cassidy twisted her watch nervously around her wrist. "Zach, I'm really worried I'm going to fail my final presentation. There's just so much information and all these stupid field trips haven't exactly been improving my language skills and . . . I just don't know what to do."

"I tried to tell her to cool the experiential crap." Zach sighed. "So what can I do to help?"

This time she twisted her watch with so much force that the clasp came undone and the silver band went clattering to the floor. "Oh, damn!" She bent quickly to pick it up. Unfortunately, Zach had the same thought at the same time and their heads collided midway down with a loud *thwack*.

"Ouch!" they cried simultaneously, standing up and rubbing their heads. Cassidy wished the polished linoleum tiles would magically part so she could disappear into them and never have to face Zach again. Her plan was simple—why was it turning out to be so hard to follow?

But when she looked up, Zach was holding out her watch and smiling.

"Obviously I need help with more than just my French," she joked, clasping the watch back onto her wrist. "I guess I could use a little tutoring on my motor skills too."

Zach laughed, shaking his head. "Tutoring, huh?" he asked. "Is that what you dragged me over here to ask me about?"

"If I recall correctly, *you're* the one who did the dragging." Cassidy's heart resumed its drum-machine beat. "But seriously, I was looking at the brochure for this program and it *did* say the TA was available for out-of-class consultations. And if I fail, my parents are *not* going to be thrilled."

"That's cool—it's what I'm here for." Zach's new Ice Man persona appeared to be melting. "Actually, I'm free right now. That is, if you are."

"Um . . ." Cassidy pretended to think. As if! She would have canceled lunch with the entire cast of *Lords of Dogtown* to study French with Zach. "Sure. Do you want to come to my place?"

"Okay," Zach said. "Mind if I catch a ride with you? Madame Briand had to commandeer the Xterra. Don't ask."

Cassidy giggled. Asking questions was the last thing on her mind.

*   *   *

They didn't talk much on the way over. Cassidy was nervous, intent on driving, and afraid to look at Zach. She zipped through the streets, maneuvering the Volvo like a sleek, zippy sports car instead of the clunky behemoth it was. Green Day blasted on the radio and she turned it up, listening to Zach drum along to the beat on her dashboard. Wind whipped through the car from the open windows, the motion of the air hardly enough to mask the fact that it was close to a hundred degrees outside. Zach's hair stuck to his forehead in the humidity, but even with a thin sheen of sweat on his upper lip he still looked gorgeous.

"Oh, well, at least my house will be air-conditioned," Cassidy joked as she cut the motor in her driveway, their feet crunching on the gravel.

But when she stepped through the front door, the air was as warm and stale as her grandmother's breath. *AC on the blink—repairman not available until tomorrow* was written on the whiteboard in her mother's anally neat handwriting.

"Damn," Cassidy said. She was reluctant to suggest they go to Zach's place—it would seem too obvious, like all she wanted to do was have sex with him again. Which she kind of did, but that was beside the point.

"It's like the fifth circle of hell in here," Zach joked. "Maybe we could hit a coffee shop or something?"

Cassidy ground her teeth in frustration. How was she supposed to confront Zach in a coffee shop, with all those people sitting around sipping iced lattes and reading the newspaper?

"Well, we have a pool out back," she suggested. "And I could, like, make us a cool drink or something too."

Zach bit his lip. Cassidy wondered if he was having some kind of inner battle over whether he should be alone with her again. But all he did was offer to make lemonade while she went upstairs to put on her swimsuit.

Cassidy gulped. She hadn't thought about the bathing suit factor, but there was no going back now. She showed Zach to the kitchen and then rushed upstairs to change, struggling through the soupy air and wishing she could just forget her whole silly plan, dive into the pool, and float there until Zach was back in New York and she could finally cool off.

She noticed the skimpy hot-pink bikini she'd bought at the end of the school year—before she realized she'd be stuck in French class all summer. She hadn't even worn it yet. Skimpy and hot pink were usually not her style, but it had been on sale and she'd been feeling adventurous. She ripped off the tags and looked at herself in the mirror, noticing that the subtle underwire made her boobs look *huge*. *Well, maybe that isn't entirely a bad thing,* she thought, throwing a sheer Donna Karan sarong around her waist so it didn't look like she was trying *too* hard.

"Wow," Zach said when she returned to the kitchen. He stared down at her body in the bikini, then quickly glanced up again. She could see his Adam's apple bobbing nervously in his neck as he squeezed a lemon wedge that missed the pitcher by several inches. Cassidy thought how funny it was that even the smartest guys could be reduced to grunting like primates the moment you showed a little skin.

"So Zach," she said, leading the way through the sliding glass doors to the backyard. She sat across from him and swished the tart, sweet lemonade across her tongue. "I could really use some help with my *French*."

Zach looked like he had fireworks going off in his head. "Cassidy?" he said uncomfortably. "No offense, but I'm going to have a lot of trouble concentrating on French with you dressed like that."

"Oh, really?" Cassidy countered. "Because after the way you've been treating me, I'm surprised you even noticed I'm here." She crossed one leg saucily over the other, gazing at him reproachfully down the length of her nose.

"I'm sorry," Zach said quietly. "I know I've been ignoring you. I guess I should explain."

"Yup," Cassidy agreed. Even though her voice sounded cool and guarded, her heart was hammering away in her chest. She couldn't believe she had actually gotten up the guts to confront him. "I guess you should."

"I think you're amazing." Zach leaned forward and looked her in the eye. "You're beautiful, you're smart and funny, and you're great to talk to. I think about you all the time, but I feel like things got out of control that night we . . . well, you know. I was trying to keep it together and make sure we didn't do anything we'd regret, but being with you just makes me . . ." He shrugged helplessly, unable to finish his sentence.

A secret smile spread through her, knowing that she had put a writer at a loss for words. That was part of what was so great about Zach—he made her feel special, as beautiful and unique as a movie star. But that didn't make up for the fact that he had probably just been using her, she reminded herself sternly. He wasn't getting off *that* easily.

"Anyway, I feel bad about it," he continued. "You're so great and I care about you so much, but I'm leaving for school in a few weeks and I just couldn't handle a long-distance relationship. It wouldn't be fair to either one of us." He sighed. "This feels so right, Cassidy, but the timing is just all wrong."

She couldn't quite put her finger on why what he was saying didn't make sense, but something was missing. "If it feels right, why shouldn't we just . . . I don't know, go with it?"

Zach picked a lemon wedge out of his drink and sucked it contemplatively. "Well, I don't want you to get hurt, first of all."

"It's nice that you care about my feelings," Cassidy said slowly. "But maybe you could have, like . . . asked me?"

Zach sighed again. "I guess you're right. But . . . I don't know, I was kind of freaked out by what happened and I figured that maybe if I just ignored it, it would go away. I guess that wasn't very mature of me, huh?"

"Not really, no," Cassidy said. For the first time, she was seeing a crack in Zach's perfectly polished veneer, an imperfection in the guy who had seemed completely perfect. "I was really upset that you weren't talking to me. It was my first time having sex with someone, and I expected to at least get acknowledged afterward." She could feel her cheeks burning.

"I'm sorry," Zach said, his head in his hands. "I'm such a jerk."

"No, you're not a jerk," she said. "But you did a jerky thing. So thanks for apologizing."

"You're welcome," Zach said. "So I guess we should just, like, chill for the rest of the summer, huh?"

"'Chill'? Why?" Cassidy asked.

"What do you mean, 'why'?" Zach said. "Because of what I said earlier. I'm going back to New York and you'll still be here. Even though I think you're great, I just can't sustain that kind of relationship."

"Haven't you ever heard of a summer romance?" Cassidy asked. "I mean, I know you're going away in a few weeks and a long-distance thing probably isn't right for either one of us, but I don't see why that means we can't be together now. I mean, I care about you too. I have fun with you. So why can't we just enjoy this while it lasts?"

She didn't have time to think about her words before they flew out of her mouth. All she knew was that she wanted to be with Zach right then—he made her feel too good to care about what would happen a few weeks down the road.

"Are you sure?" Zach said. "I just don't want you to get hurt."

"I won't," Cassidy assured him. "Or if I do, I don't know—I guess I can handle that."

"Positive?" Zach said. "Because you look so good in that bikini, I might have to take advantage of this in about thirty seconds."

"Positive," Cassidy said.

"Twenty-nine," Zach teased. "Twenty-eight . . ."

Cassidy leaned forward and kissed him. They never got to twenty-seven.

Chapter Nineteen

Text message from Eric, 5:19 p.m., Aug. 23: Im
over you
Text message from Eric, 5:24 p.m., Aug. 23:
Miss you. Call me.

"Who keeps texting you?" Zach asked, shifting so the
beanbag chair made a soft swishing noise.

"Just an old friend." Cassidy clicked her cell phone
to vibrate and shoved it under her pillow, thinking that
she really should call Eric later that night just to check
in. They were supposed to be friends, she reminded herself. But she would deal with that later. For now, she had
an important study session to attend to.

She turned to Zach. "Where was I?" she asked.

"You were talking about Monet's 'Water Lilies'," Zach reminded her.

"Oh, yeah." Cassidy took a deep breath and launched back into her presentation, trying not to glance at the index cards Zach had helped her make, which were spread out across the bed. Practicing in front of Zach made everything easier. She felt like she was learning more in the afternoons with him than she had in an entire summer of classes with Madame Briand. Plus Zach's special technique to help her get over her fear of public speaking was a *lot* more fun than anything they'd done in class.

"Hey!" Zach interrupted suddenly. "You messed up there, Cass. Your noun and verb didn't agree. You know what that means."

Cassidy giggled. "But I don't have much left to lose," she said. She stood in front of him in her bra, panties, and one sandal.

"Then maybe you should make fewer mistakes," Zach teased. "Besides, practicing au naturel is good for you. If you can do your presentation naked, speaking in front of a whole class with your clothes on will be no sweat."

"If I didn't give you so much credit as a teacher, I'd say you had some kind of ulterior motive." Cassidy laughed, bending to unbuckle her sandal.

"Motive? Me? Never." Zach grinned. "I just want to

see you ace this presentation, that's all. Now, weren't you in the middle of saying something important about art?"

Cassidy tried to compose herself, but the moment she started talking, Zach stuck out his tongue and wiggled it around in the air so that she broke down again in giggles.

"No giggling!" Zach called. "Time to lose the bra!"

"But that's not fair," Cassidy protested. "You *made* me crack up."

"There will be distractions in the classroom," Zach reminded her. "It's up to *you* to maintain control no matter what's going on. But I'll be nice—I'll help you with the clasp."

"I still can't help thinking you're getting something out of this too," Cassidy mused, crouching down in front of him so Zach could unhook her bra. He turned her around, still laughing, and kissed her lightly on the mouth. Cassidy had a feeling it was going to be a while before she got to the end of her speech, but she was too happy kissing Zach to care.

*   *   *

Cassidy could barely sit still behind her desk. She glanced at the clock just as it ticked loudly and advanced to 10:13 A.M. Just six hours and seventeen minutes until she and Zach could be alone together! Factoring in the drive, that was a little over six hours until his shirt would be on her bedroom floor and the baby-smooth skin of his back under her hands. Cassidy wriggled in her chair at the thought.

Ever since their reconciliation at her pool, life had taken on a hazy, glimmering sheen. Cassidy felt physically lighter, her limbs warm and loose, as if she'd been huddling against an invisible cold that had finally given way to a dazzling springtime. Her mind was wrapped around Zach 24/7—and so was her body, whenever they had the chance. She had never felt this way about Eric. In fact, she had never felt this way about *anyone*, and it was the most wonderful feeling in the world.

Zach was draped over a chair in the front of the room. He turned around to survey the class. His eyes rested on hers for a long moment as a molasses-slow smile played across his face. He didn't wink. He didn't need to. There was so much energy zinging through the air between them that Cassidy was surprised the rest of the class couldn't feel it too.

There was a timid knock on the classroom door, and Cassidy automatically sat up straighter in her chair as Madame Briand sang out (in French, of course) for whomever was knocking to enter. A clerk who Cassidy vaguely recognized from the admissions office scurried in and whispered something in Madame Briand's ear.

"Oh, *mon Dieu!*" Madame Briand gasped. Then she looked at Zach. "You have a phone call in the office," she told him.

Cassidy felt chills shoot through her limbs. People only got phone calls in offices when things were serious—like a disease or a death in the family. Her heart went out to Zach, but he didn't turn to look at her. He was already following the clerk out the door and down the hall.

Cassidy spent the next fifteen minutes in agony, envisioning every possible gory scenario. When the door swung open again, the entire class swiveled their heads toward it. Zach strolled in, not looking like he'd just gotten news of a death or an unwanted pregnancy. In fact, he was smiling.

"*C'est rien,*" he told the class. *It's nothing.* But his smile flickered when he looked at Cassidy, then faded entirely. And somehow she knew that whatever the phone call had been about affected *them*.

There was no way she could just sit there and listen to Madame Briand prattle on about the weather in Normandy with all this going through her mind. She was probably getting upset over nothing, but she needed to chill out. She raised her hand and excused herself to the bathroom.

Cassidy was halfway down the hall when she heard footsteps behind her. Whirling around, she saw Zach running to catch up and nearly sank to her knees in gratitude that he'd been so quick to read her mind.

"What's going on?" she said, wrapping her arms around him after glancing quickly up and down the hallway to make sure they were alone.

Zach stroked her hair and looked into her eyes. "It's good news for me," he said. "But not so good for us. You know how I told you I was a junior RA my freshman year?"

Cassidy nodded, wondering what that had to do with her. "Well," he continued, "one of the senior RAs just dropped out, and they need someone to replace him right away. It's great for me because I get free room and board—but it means I have to leave early tomorrow morning. Training has already started."

For a moment, Cassidy was unable to process the information. "Leave?" was all she could manage to say.

"Leave Malibu," he confirmed grimly. "Fly to New York. For the year."

"Oh." Her voice echoed hollowly in the hallway.

"Cassidy, I'm sorry." He brought her in for a tight hug. "I know things were just getting good between us. I was enjoying this as much as you were, but you know I have to do this."

"I understand," she said flatly. She'd known from the beginning that he would leave sooner or later, but why did it have to be now?

Zach disentangled himself and looked around guiltily, worried someone had seen them embrace. But nobody had. "Listen, I need to get back to class," he said. "But I want to spend every moment I can with you afterward. I even want you to drive me to the airport tomorrow morning if that's okay—I have to drop the Xterra off at Avis. You can tell Madame Briand you have a dentist appointment or something. She's so flaky, she won't know the difference anyway."

Cassidy nodded miserably. She watched his slow, rolling gait as he walked back to class before running to the ladies' room, locking herself in a stall, and bursting into tears.

So much for having changed: She felt like the same old Cassidy, always crying in bathroom stalls. How was she supposed to sit through six hours of French class knowing that Zach was about to get on a plane and fly three thousand miles away from her? Nothing could have prepared her for how much it hurt.

As she tossed another ball of snotty toilet paper into the bowl below her, she almost wished she'd listened to Zach and stopped what was happening between them before she got too attached. The whole temporary-summer-romance thing had made their relationship more romantic, but now that the "temporary" part was a reality, it hurt like nothing had ever hurt before. The continuous sunny day her summer had become with Zach in her life was suddenly cold, gray, and drizzly. And he hadn't even left yet! She had to stifle a sniffle as the door to the bathroom creaked open and a small pair of heels clattered tentatively on the tile floor.

"Cassidy?"

"Yeah?" she replied, hoping the tears weren't coming through in her voice.

"It's Cecilia. You were gone for a long time, so Madame Briand wanted me to come and see if you were okay."

Cassidy struggled to think of some excuse for spending the past half hour in the bathroom. The last thing she needed was for the teacher's pet to find out she'd been getting it on with the TA. "Well, this is kind of embarrassing. Do you happen to have a tampon?"

"Oh!" Cecilia gasped. "No, but there's a machine out here. I could put a quarter in it for you."

"Could you?" Cassidy asked as sweetly as she could.

"Sure, no problem," Cecilia said. Cassidy heard the clink of coins on metal and the rustling of a plastic-coated wrapper, which emerged seconds later under the door to her stall.

"Thanks," she said gratefully. "I really appreciate it, Cecilia."

"No problem," Cecilia said, sounding relieved that she didn't have to perform CPR or anything else lifesaving. "So, see you back in class? She's going over the vocab quiz and I really don't want to miss it."

"Go," Cassidy urged. "And thanks a million. Really."

As soon as Cecilia was gone, she tossed the unused tampon in the garbage, emerged from the stall, and splashed cold water on her face to make the swelling come down. She'd never thought Cecilia would be good for much of anything, but at least she'd gotten Cassidy's mind off the Zach situation long enough for her to stop crying.

She was feeling almost confident when she reentered the classroom, shooting an apologetic glance to Madame Briand and sharing a knowing smile with Cecilia. But then her eyes landed on Zach and she knew it would be the last time she'd ever walk into a classroom and see him sitting there, and she almost started crying all over again.

The next few hours were torture. There was no way she could concentrate on the lesson. All she could think about was how Zach-less her life was going to be and how much of the summer they'd wasted before letting what was going on between them happen. If only they had kissed that first day in the sculpture garden, if only she'd confronted him sooner after they had sex, if only she'd known she was in love with him the moment she saw him, they could have had all those extra days together. But then wouldn't it have hurt even more when he had to leave? There was no way of knowing. All she knew was that she was losing him forever.

* * *

Later that night, Cassidy sat on Zach's bed with her back against the wall and her knees drawn up to her chin, watching him transfer musty-smelling jeans from a dresser drawer into the large suitcase propped open next to her. She was tired of watching him pack; everything he put in the suitcase seemed to bring him another step closer to New York and farther away from her. She reached over to turn up the CD he'd picked to pack to, some DJ from a club in Ibiza spinning break beats, not so much because she wanted to hear the music as because she didn't want to talk.

No, it wasn't that she didn't *want* to talk. She wished more than anything that she knew what to say. But she was afraid that if she opened her mouth, she'd start screaming at him for leaving her when she'd known it was bound to happen all along. She didn't want to sound as juvenile and desperate as she felt.

Zach put the pile of jeans down on the bed and sat close to her, taking her hands in his. "Are you okay?"

"Yeah." Cassidy nodded. "I'm fine. Just a little . . . you know."

Zach leaned over to turn the music down. She could feel the tears welling up inside her again. She felt like they hadn't stopped since she first found out he was leaving but had been pouring down her insides for the past few hours so that now they were all dammed up somewhere beneath her heart, just waiting for the right opportunity to spill out.

And she knew that Zach could read it on her face.

"Come here," he said, spreading his arms. She dove face-first into him, huddling against his chest as sobs racked her body.

"It's just that I'll miss you so much," she said when she finally caught her breath.

"I know," Zach said, his lips against her ear, his voice soothing and hypnotic. "I'll miss you too, Cassidy. Don't think this isn't painful for me too."

"But you're the one who gets to go away to a whole new place," Cassidy whined. She knew she sounded childish, but she couldn't seem to help it. "I'll be stuck here, and everything will be the same. At least having you around made things sort of interesting."

Zach cupped her face in his hands and she shivered at his touch. "Things won't really be the same because *you'll* be different. And when you're different, the whole world around you changes too. You see it through a new set of eyes."

"Have I really changed that much?" Cassidy asked. At the moment, she felt even younger than she had when she and Zach had first met. More vulnerable. More likely to burst into tears like an overtired toddler who'd spent too many hours being dragged through a department store.

"Yes," Zach said firmly. "When I first met you, Cass,

you could barely talk to anyone. Now you're like a social butterfly. Remember the way you cracked Larissa's friends up at the fashion show?"

Cassidy nodded.

"That's not something the Cassidy Jones I first met would have been able to do," Zach said. "When I first met you, Cass, you were afraid to even speak to me. You have no idea how much I've watched you grow in this short time."

"But what if I'm only that way around you?" Cassidy asked. "What if the second you leave, everything goes back to the way it was?"

Zach moved closer to her on the bed and put his arm around her shoulders. "Well, you can let that happen if you want. Or you can have faith in yourself to keep on learning and growing."

"I guess you're right." Cassidy sighed, snuggling against his shoulder.

The CD ended and silence filled the room. She could feel Zach's pulse against her cheek.

"I'll never forget this summer," he whispered. "Or you."

Cassidy sighed again. Zach drew her in closer and their lips met, tentatively at first but growing more and more urgent. Cassidy knew as she tugged her shirt above her head that this would be the last time she and Zach would ever do this, and she tried to drink in as much of him as possible, to imprint his smell and the feel of his skin in her memory in indelible ink. She could feel the piles of shirts he'd stacked neatly on the bed sliding away from them as he climbed on top of her, and the loud thump of his suitcase hitting the floor was enough to make them pause for a moment but not to stop. Cassidy wanted to hold him just like that forever, hovering over her, his ragged breaths matching hers, both of them afraid to move much for fear it would be over too soon. She wanted to take those few moments and freeze them in a test tube so she could go back and revisit them every day for the rest of her life. Most of all, she just wanted Zach to stay there in Malibu, with her.

Her cheeks were wet with tears when they finished. Zach bent to kiss them gently away before gathering her in his arms and holding her tightly as they drifted off to sleep.

*   *   *

The jarring bleep of the alarm clock woke them up. Zach groaned and flailed his hand in its direction, obviously hoping it would land on snooze but missing by about a foot.

Cassidy sat up quickly, confused. The sky outside the window was still dark. She reached over, turned off the alarm clock, and looked down at Zach. He had drifted back into sleep, and his face against the pillow looked as content and innocent as a child's. Cassidy took a silent mental snapshot before gently shaking him awake.

"It's still dark out," Zach moaned as his eyes blinked open.

"You have to catch your plane," Cassidy reminded him, feeling sick to her stomach as she uttered the words.

Zach bolted upright. "Shit, what time is it?" he asked, looking around wildly.

Cassidy pointed to the clock.

"I have to finish packing." Zach scrambled out of bed and into a pair of black boxer-briefs he found under the overturned suitcase on the floor. Cassidy sat up and pulled the covers around her chin as she watched him hurriedly toss the rest of his clothing into the suitcase and struggle to zip it up. Her mouth tasted like she'd been chewing sawdust, and she had a headache. She felt hungover, even though she hadn't had anything to drink the night before.

Zach disappeared into the bathroom and returned shaking water droplets from a toothbrush, which he shoved into the pocket of his duffel bag.

"Ready?" he asked, leaning down to kiss Cassidy on the forehead. She got out of bed and struggled into her clothes. Her skin felt sticky from not showering.

He lifted the suitcase and duffel bag, and she silently shouldered an oversized backpack, which she carried out to the driveway and heaved into the trunk of the Volvo. Zach began to fiddle with the radio once they were on the road, wrinkling his nose as he spun the dial furiously through the FM stations. By the time they got to the departures terminal, Cassidy estimated they must have listened to about four seconds each of fifty songs, and about a hundred commercials.

"This is me," Zach said, leaning forward and pointing through the windshield to a big brown Delta sign. Cassidy's heart felt like lead as she pulled up to the curb and got out to help him with his bags. Once they were all stacked on the curb, Zach turned to face her.

"I really will miss you," he said, his voice heavy with emotion.

"I'll miss you too." Cassidy willed herself not to cry. If there was a time to be strong, she thought, this was it.

"We'll always have Malibu," Zach joked, and they both tried to smile. Cassidy didn't know what else to say. She wanted to tell him that she loved him and would never forget him as long as she lived, but the words stuck in her throat. You weren't supposed to say "I love you" to your summer fling, were you?

Fortunately, she didn't have to say anything at all. Zach leaned down and gave her a long, lingering kiss. When he straightened, she could almost see tears glimmering in his eyes.

"I have to go," he said, definitely choked up. "Take

care of yourself, okay?"

"Good-bye," she said quietly.

She watched as he balanced the three bags around his body and sauntered through the automatic sliding glass doors, into the terminal, and out of her life forever.

She navigated the complicated ramps and byways around the airport on automatic pilot, thankful that the early-morning traffic was nearly nonexistent. It was just starting to get light out, and as she sped down the freeway, she decided that home was the very last place she wanted to go. She felt like she needed about a million years of sleep but was afraid that once she crawled into her bed, she would never get out again.

Instead she found herself taking an exit off the freeway that led to the beach. The sky was just starting to brighten as she pulled into the empty parking lot, and she thought sitting on the sand and watching the sun come up might make her feel better.

Cassidy took off her shoes and stepped onto the beach, shivering slightly at the cool touch of the sand against her feet. It must have rained while she and Zach were sleeping because the beach felt wet and soggy and the waves roared below her like they were dissatisfied with the world. Cassidy walked halfway down to where the surf hit the sand and sat, feeling the dampness soak through her skirt and into her skin. She wrapped her arms around herself and rocked back and forth, waiting for dawn's gentle colors to break through the clouds above her.

But the sky was gray and overcast, and even the keening of the seagulls seemed lonely and sad. Instead of cheering her up, the day seemed determined to reflect how she was feeling.

And the way she was feeling was empty. Torn apart. Like there was something missing inside her and nothing would ever be the same again.

Chapter Twenty

Dear Cassidy,

    I don't know what to say. I hope you're all right. I wish I was there. If it makes you feel any better (not that it will), I'll be home in less than a week and I promise when I am, I'll do as much to distract you as possible.

    Actually, I guess I can start now. Want to know something really ironic? Yesterday when we were done with afternoon group, this guy Jesse asked if I wanted to take a walk with him. I've never told you about him because he never says anything at all, he usually just kind of sits there like a bump on a log, so I was pretty surprised, but I didn't have anything better to do so I went with him. We walked down to

*the lake and then he took out this joint and was like,
"Wanna smoke?"*

*And I figured, you know what? Here I am in god-
damn rehab and I've never even tried it. I might as well
at least know what it's like. So I shared this joint with
Jesse. You wouldn't believe what it did! First it made me
sleepy. Then it made me hungry. And that was it! I have
no clue what the big deal is. Do you? I'm going to have
to give my brother some serious hell for being so into such
a pointless drug when I get home.*

*I hope that cheered you up a little. I'm looking for-
ward to seeing you again.*

Joe

It sucked. There was no other way for Cassidy to
describe the way she'd been feeling since Zach had left.
And it didn't suck the way losing your cell phone or getting grounded for a couple of days sucked. It sucked like
having a vacuum cleaner attached to your heart and trying to pull it out of your chest, sucked all the fun and
freedom and sunlight from her life, sucked like watching
your dog get put to sleep. That kind of suck.

And the only thing she could do about it was stay in
bed and cry.

Cassidy knew it was dumb and awful to get so bent
out of shape over a guy, but Zach hadn't been *just a guy*.

Zach was the hottest, most brilliant guy in the world. The guy she'd chosen to lose her virginity to. The guy who was three thousand miles away in New York City and hadn't called once since he'd left.

After the second day of sneaking out of French class every half hour to check her messages and coming home right after class to climb into bed, watch the Lifetime channel, and sniffle into a box of tissues, Cassidy remembered an old record her dad used to play sometimes when she was a kid. While her parents were out that evening at a dinner party, she crept downstairs to the den and flipped through the dusty record jackets her dad kept in a little-used cabinet behind the gleaming new entertainment center. When she found what she was looking for, she brought the record up to her room, then came back for the turntable, which she had to struggle to keep from dropping on the stairs.

It was worth it, though. The snaps and crackles on the old album seemed like the perfect background for the song, which she played over and over again, quickly learning how to set the needle back into the proper groove.

Maybe I should start spinning at clubs, Cassidy thought bitterly as Al Green began to sing again:

Ain't no sunshine when she's gone,
A-woah-a-woah-woah.
Only darkness every day.

In her head, she substituted *he* for *she*. Because that was exactly how she felt: like Zach's going away had left a permanent stain across the sun, and her world would never be bright again.

"What the hell is this crap?" a voice said somewhere in her room. Cassidy couldn't tell exactly where because she had the covers pulled over her head and was rocking back and forth to the music.

"Go away," she said automatically.

Cassidy flinched as a hand reached down and yanked the covers off her, flooding her eyes with light.

"Wow, dude," said Larissa, standing over her with the blankets in one hand and her oversize neon green Emilio Pucci tote bag in the other. "I came to try and win you back as my best friend, but it looks like I may need to give you a makeover first. When was the last time you brushed your hair?"

"Hair?" Cassidy's hand went gingerly to her head. It felt a little crunchy, but not too bad. "I don't remember. It doesn't matter. I'm too depressed to think about it."

"How long have you been wallowing?" Larissa asked. "Because if it's been more than two days, your official wallowing period is over. Come on, Cass. How about we put some highlights in your hair or something to cheer you up?"

"I don't know," Cassidy said. "Considering what you said the last time I saw you, how do I know you won't try to turn my hair green?"

"Well, you know, that's part of the reason I came here," Larissa said, shifting nervously from foot to foot.

"To turn my hair green?" Cassidy asked.

"No!" Larissa corrected her quickly. "I mean, I know I was a total *bee-otch* last time we hung out and, like . . ." Cassidy could see her struggling to get the words out. "I wanted to apologize."

"Really?" Cassidy asked. Larissa almost never apologized for anything.

Larissa bit her lip and nodded firmly. "Yeah. I was just so embarrassed about what happened at the show, and I took it out on you, which was mega-unfair. I'm so, *so* sorry."

"Wow," Cassidy said. "It's very un-Larissa-like of you to admit you were wrong."

"I know," Larissa said sheepishly. "I'm trying to change. I realized after a while that I missed talking to you."

"I missed talking to you too," Cassidy said. "But when I tried to tell you that, you didn't seem to want to listen."

"I know." Larissa looked guiltily down at the floor. "I just got so wrapped up in the whole fashion-show thing and all my new friends and, like, you were acting all weird and stuff."

"Me? How was I acting weird?" Cassidy asked.

"You know: doing crazy things like actually talking to people when we went out. It just kind of threw me off guard. But you weren't obnoxious at all. I was. Seriously. Everyone liked you a lot."

"It seemed like you kind of had a problem with that," Cassidy said.

Larissa sighed and looked down at her sparkly green fingernails. "This is going to sound retarded," she said. "But I kind of felt threatened by you."

"You're right, that is retarded."

"I mean it. Here you were, talking about sophisticated stuff that I knew nothing about and making jokes I didn't even get. I just wasn't used to feeling like the outsider. It made me feel so self-conscious."

"I understand what you mean," Cassidy said. "That's exactly how I used to feel."

"I never realized how icky that is, to be worried about talking and everything. What a drag."

"It was. But I'm working on being more outgoing, and I'm liking it a lot."

"Really? So you're going to be more like me?" Larissa asked excitedly.

"I said outgoing, not outlandish," Cassidy quipped.

"Again with the jokes. I got that one, though. You're pretty funny for a sidekick," Larissa said, smiling. "So do you forgive me?"

"Of course I do," Cassidy said. "I wouldn't want to ruin this season finale moment of ours."

"Thank God." Larissa laughed. "But it's not over yet. You have to tell me what you're doing lying around in a dark room crying on a beautiful day."

"Oh, this," Cassidy said, looking down at her dirty oversize T-shirt and badly chewed fingernails. "This is the work of a boy."

"Eric?" Larissa gasped.

"Wow. It really *has* been a long time since we talked."

"*Not* Eric? I think I need to sit down." Larissa dragged Cassidy's beanbag chair toward the bed and sat with her elbows on her knees and her chin in her hands, looking at Cassidy questioningly.

Cassidy found herself telling Larissa the whole story—how she and Eric had broken up and the disastrous effect of Zach coming into her life. How she'd been scared of her feelings toward him but unable to resist them at the same time. How they'd tried to avoid hooking up for so long, but when it happened, it had felt so right and inevitable and then how terrible it had been breaking up with Eric. When she got to the part about losing her virginity, Larissa yelped and clapped her hand to her mouth.

"I can't believe you actually did it!" she squealed. "So you lost it to him and then—what, he dumped you? What a jerk!"

"Not exactly. He went back to school in New York and . . . well, you know."

"He 'just couldn't handle the distance thing'?" Larissa air-quoted.

She was so right on that Cassidy had to laugh.

"That's the worst." Larissa sighed. "I just read this article in *Cosmo* about how something like ninety percent of summer romances end that way. I wish I'd been around to warn you."

"I wish you had too!" Cassidy said. "It would have saved me a lot of grief."

"Well, sometimes you have to be kicked in the ass," Larissa said. "But I have something that'll make you feel better. Give this a go." She pulled a large roll of what looked like Saran Wrap from her oversize tote.

"What is that?" Cassidy asked. Larissa unrolled the Saran Wrap, which turned out to be full of air bubbles.

"Pop some," she commanded, handing it to Cassidy.

"You want me to pop bubble wrap?" Cassidy asked. "Why?" She didn't want to pop bubble wrap. She wanted to fly to New York City and make out with Zach!

"You'll see," Larissa urged. "Just try one."

"Fine." Cassidy pressed her thumb down on one of the air pockets and squeezed.

Pop!

It *did* feel good. Cassidy squeezed another and felt it

explode under her fingers, then began popping more and more quickly. It seemed like with every pop, the knot in her heart loosened a tiny bit. Before she knew it, she'd demolished the sheet Larissa had given her, and her entire body felt lighter.

"You think that's good." Larissa smiled, reaching into her tote again. "Try *this*."

She pulled out another, larger sheet with air bubbles twice the size. It took Cassidy both thumbs to pop just one.

"What is this, industrial grade?" she asked.

"If you're having trouble . . ." Larissa continued, removing a hammer from her tote.

Cassidy cracked up even as she took the hammer in her hands. She placed the bubble wrap on her bed and slammed it so hard that her plush rhinoceros went flying.

"Feel better?" Larissa asked.

"Yes!" Cassidy screamed over the exploding bubbles, swinging the hammer with all her might. She missed the bubble wrap by a good six inches and collapsed in a pile on her bed, laughing. She couldn't believe how good it felt to get some of the negative energy out. She'd been crying so much over the past few days she had started to think she would never laugh again. "Got any more?" she asked, sitting up and smoothing her hair away from her face.

"All out." Larissa shrugged. She found her tote bag on the floor and began pulling things out of it. "But I have something else that does wonders for a broken heart."

"What, an industrial-size bottle of Captain Morgan?" Cassidy joked.

"No," Larissa said, triumphantly producing a shiny box with a picture of a woman smiling from the cover. The woman had brown hair laced with stunning gold highlights. "This."

"A home highlighting kit?" Cassidy asked dubiously.

"Exactly. New Cassidy, new hair. Makes sense, right?"

Cassidy looked at the box. It could be fun, and she wouldn't mind a different look for the beginning of the school year. Now that she was done being a wallflower, maybe her hair should reflect that.

"Okay," she said finally. "I'll do it. Only this time, we're trying a test patch first to make sure I'm not allergic."

"Not like last time," Larissa said solemnly before they both burst into the longest, loudest, most freeing bout of laughter Cassidy had ever had.

Chapter Twenty-One

From: zbw206@nyu.edu
Sent: September 1
To: Cassidy.Jones@gmail.com
Re: Good luck!

Hey, Cassidy,
Just wanted to wish you good luck on your French presentation. I know you can do it! Just remember all those times you did it for me in your undies and you'll be all set ;).

New York is fine. I'm happy to be here. I was getting kind of antsy in Malibu—not because of you, though. We writers just have to keep on the move, always seeking out the next adventure.

Stay well,
Zach

Cassidy woke on the morning of her presentation already sweating and feeling nauseous. She couldn't believe she had to get up in front of nearly twenty people and speak in French for ten whole minutes about impressionist art. She considered crawling back under the covers and never coming out again, but she knew that wasn't really an option. *Might as well get it over with,* she thought as she climbed out of bed and into the shower.

By the time she got to school, though, she was a nervous wreck. She kept wiping her palms down the length of her skirt, hoping the sweat wouldn't show against the conservative plaid pattern she'd picked out. She'd checked her bag to make sure her notes were there at least sixteen times, but seeing the index cards held neatly together with a small red rubber band didn't make her feel any better. As her kitten heels clicked down the hallway, she had to physically resist an urge to duck into the ladies' room and hide there until the class was over.

"Nervous?" Benjy asked as she sat down next to him.

"Nervous? Not me!" she said, wondering if he could hear the tremor in her voice.

"Liar," he teased. "I'm shitting myself, so I know *you're* nervous."

"And just what is *that* supposed to mean?" Cassidy asked, arching an eyebrow. At least kidding around with Benjy was taking her mind momentarily off the dread knotting its way through her stomach.

"Is everyone ready?" Madame Briand asked in French, her eyes glittering with excitement. To her, final presentations were a *fun learning experience*. Maybe because she was *completely delusional*, Cassidy thought.

"Now, who wants to go first?" she asked, looking straight at Cecilia before she even had a chance to raise her hand. Cecilia leapt up from her seat and bounced to the front of the room. She unrolled a large piece of poster board and stuck it to the wall. Great. Not only did Cecilia have eleven-and-a-half minutes of solid facts about the French economy, she had also drawn a *graph*.

When she finished, Madame Briand burst into applause. The rest of the class reluctantly followed. Cecilia grinned like she'd just won the Nobel Peace Prize.

"And who is next?" Madame Briand asked, looking around for hands that didn't go up. Nobody wanted to follow an act like Cecilia's. Silence filled the room as everybody shifted their eyes from the person sitting next to them to their own shoes on the floor, avoiding Madame Briand's gaze and hoping that she wouldn't pick them.

In the silence, Cassidy realized that the sooner she got this over with, the sooner she would be able to stop worrying about her French presentation for the rest of her life. So she raised her hand.

"Cassidy!" Madame Briand gasped, clearly trying to hide her surprise. Cassidy felt her stomach recoil. What had she been thinking? She got to her feet slowly, her pulse pounding in her temples. As she stood up, the classroom whirled around her. *Chill,* she commanded herself. *It'll be over soon.*

As she walked to the front of the room, her hands so damp they were smudging the neat writing on her index cards, Cassidy wondered if the rest of the class could see her shaking. She felt like she was standing in the middle of the Arctic Circle in the wintertime wearing nothing but her underwear. And then she remembered the way Zach had her take off her clothes when she practiced for him, the grin on his face when he said that if she could do it in her underwear, she could do anything. She felt his smile spread to her own face.

Cassidy placed her note cards on the podium, took a deep, shuddering breath, and began. At first, her voice came out as a squeak, so high-pitched she could barely hear it in her own ears. She cleared her throat and began again.

"When France the nation was reborn as an atheist," she said in French, and paused. She'd meant to say reborn as an *artist*, not an atheist. She winced but kept going. Probably nobody would even notice.

Then she realized she had just called the king a bird. Who knew buckling knees could make it so hard to pronounce things? Then again, who cared? She knew she was flubbing every other word, but she slogged on. As she talked, she noticed the class shifting uncomfortably in their seats. When she accidentally recited a whole paragraph in the conditional instead of the past tense, Cecilia giggled outright. Cassidy stiffened. *"Et la merde de Picasso,"* she continued, and the entire class cracked up. Madame Briand looked like she'd just been socked in the head. Had Cassidy really just referred to Picasso's mother as his *shit*?

Who cared? She was doing it. She drew another long, ragged breath and stumbled through the final paragraph so quickly the words all ran together, masking both her pronunciation and her inability to correctly conjugate a single word. She spit it all out, grabbed her index cards off the podium, and looked around the room. Everyone was staring at her, dumbfounded. Cecilia wrinkled her nose in a way that suggested Cassidy should be turned into escargot feed.

A single clap echoed from the back of the room. Followed by another. And another. Cassidy looked up to see Benjy slowly bringing his hands together, a determined smile on his face. Gradually the rest of the class joined in.

"*Merci,*" Cassidy said, practically running back to her seat. "Did that suck?" she whispered in Benjy's ear.

"Totally," he whispered back. "But at least you're done."

"Right," Cassidy said, suddenly dizzy with a sense of accomplishment. So what if her presentation had sucked? She'd been the brave, new Cassidy, and that was what mattered. "It's over," she whispered to herself, loving the sound of the words as they rolled off her tongue.

*   *   *

"I'm *ba-ack!*" he said in a high-pitched, silly voice like the Joker when she picked up her phone.

"Joe!" Cassidy screamed into the receiver. "You're really home?"

"Just two doors down," Joe said. "I'm not unpacked yet, but I'd like to see you."

"I want to see you too."

"So come over," Joe said. "I'll be up in the tree house, trying to slowly acclimate myself back to life in the real world."

"Okay. See you in five!" Cassidy flipped her phone shut and was about to run out the door when she caught sight of herself in her bedroom mirror. Her new blond highlights would look even better if she brushed her hair first, she decided. And while she was at it, maybe she should brush her teeth and put on some lip gloss too. . . .

Joe probably hasn't seen a girl without twigs in her hair all summer, she told herself. That's why she was making herself look nice. But it didn't explain the tiny nervous flutter in her stomach, which increased as she walked around the side of his house.

"I'm here!" she called, shielding her eyes from the sun's mid-afternoon glare as she looked up into the branches of the giant oak. Sure enough, the familiar Chuck Taylors dangled from the entrance, and a voice called for her to come on up.

"You sound different," Cassidy said as she grabbed the bottom rung of the ladder. His voice was deeper somehow, more mature.

"It's the fresh mountain air," he replied. "Good for the vocal cords. Or some such crap."

Cassidy couldn't suppress a gasp when she reached the top of the ladder and crawled inside. Joe didn't just *sound* different—he *looked* different too. The Idaho sun had bronzed his skin gold, and his gangly limbs, which she'd remembered as being so skinny and white they almost glowed, were toned and muscular from hiking and trail work. But the most astonishing difference was in his face. It wasn't just the killer tan and chiseled jaw.

There was a spark of wisdom in Joe's eyes that hadn't been there before, and they seemed to shine with knowledge and compassion.

"Wow," Cassidy couldn't help saying. "You look amazing."

"Don't I always?" he joked, pretending to be offended.

"No, it's just . . ."

"I know," Joe said. "I don't look albino anymore. You don't have to explain."

Cassidy laughed. Just being around Joe for a few seconds made her feel relaxed and comfortable, like she didn't have to try and impress him or be on guard about what she said. He'd been reading her letters all summer and he knew exactly who she was.

"You look good too," Joe said. "I really like what you did with your hair."

"Thanks. I finally got a makeover from Larissa that actually works for me," Cassidy joked. "Oh, here. I brought you a welcome-home present." Joe's eyes lit up when she handed him a box of Cadbury Creme Eggs. "Thanks for saving my life this summer. I don't know what I would have done without you."

"You would have been fine," Joe said as he eagerly unwrapped the brightly colored foil. "Trust me, you would have figured everything out on your own. I had faith in you."

"I think that's exactly what I needed," Cassidy said. "Someone to have faith in me. Someone to just be there and tell me everything would be okay."

"I was hardly *there*," Joe pointed out. "I mean, I was several states away."

"I know; how ironic is that?" Cassidy said. "You were pretty far away, but sometimes you felt like my closest friend. Like when I called you freaking out about my face the night of my anniversary with Eric?"

"It wasn't really your face you were freaking out about," Joe said.

"True, but you helped me figure that out. I mean, even if you hadn't, it was just so great of you to talk me down that night."

"Hey, that's what I'm here for," Joe said. "People freak out. It's normal. People freaked out at Camp Crackhead all the time. I kind of got used to it—although dealing with your freak-out was way more pleasant than talking Lloyd out of killing a counselor so that he could go to jail and become a big-time dealer's bitch and get some good drugs for a change."

"That's the weirdest compliment I've ever gotten," Cassidy said. "I think I'm going to use that as my yearbook quote."

"What? I thought we both vowed to use 'let it pee.'"

Cassidy giggled at the memory of singing with Joe in sixth-grade chorus. "Oh, my God, why did we think it was *so funny* when we sang 'let it pee' instead of 'let it be'? I haven't thought of that in ages."

She had missed Joe, she realized. Not just over the summer, but for the past few years. Joe snorted a little as he laughed. Cassidy couldn't explain why it sounded sort of cute.

"So did Camp Crackhead end up being as awful as you expected?"

"Even worse." Joe laughed. "Sometimes I thought I would be stuck in a moldy cabin in Idaho for the rest of my life. But I guess it ended up being worth it in the end. It was, like, a 'growth experience' or something."

Cassidy laughed and unwrapped an egg, letting the chocolate melt slowly in her mouth. Leaves rustled against the roof of the tree house, and the smell of cut grass wafted up from the lawn. Even the shadows falling across her bare ankles seemed like they were in the perfect place.

"How about for you?" Joe asked. "I know your life was pretty turbulent for a while there, but did things turn out as bad as you expected?"

"I guess not," she said. "I mean, so much happened. I was friends with Larissa and then I wasn't, I was dating Eric and then I wasn't, and then I was dating Zach and then I wasn't. It feels like it all happened so fast."

"That's how I feel about—I don't know, everything," Joe said. "In a split second, your entire life can change."

Cassidy leaned back against the rough wooden walls of the tree house and stretched her legs out in front of her. Her ankle brushed against Joe's and she left it there, feeling the fine golden hairs on his legs tickling her skin.

"Hey, I have something for you too," Joe said around a mouthful of Cadbury chocolate. He reached under a pillow and brought out a present wrapped in plain green paper and tied with twine, which he held out shyly toward her.

Cassidy gently eased her thumb under the tape. "You didn't have to wrap it."

"But I wanted to."

Joe smiled expectantly as Cassidy peeled the wrapping off to reveal a small paperback book.

"The Meaning of Mindfulness," she read, turning it over in her hands. A tiny, elderly Tibetan monk with twinkling eyes smiled at her from the cover. The book smelled of wood smoke and pine tar. It was obviously the same copy Joe had read alone in the wilderness.

"This book helped change my life," Joe said. "I hope it'll help you too."

Cassidy didn't say anything. She just threw her arms around his neck. She meant for the hug to last only a second and be a friendly way of saying "thank you," but she held on for a little longer and tighter, thinking of all the good times she and Joe had together back in middle school and how she wanted to have more times like that with him. She remembered how he had been there for her over the summer, all the wonderful things he had said and how he had tried to keep her grounded when she thought she might come undone.

"I missed you," she whispered in his ear.

"I missed you too," he said quietly. "But I'm here now."

Looking back, it wasn't the hug that stayed fresh in Cassidy's mind. It was how she felt when she gazed into Joe's eyes. A new year was ahead of her, and it was as if there were no more secrets for her to uncover. She'd found out everything she needed to know.

Do you want to find true love? Better throw away that map! Here's an excerpt from Hailey Abbott's

GETTING LOST WITH BOYS

Cordelia scrubbed herself furiously with Origins Pomegranate Wash. Not only was her mind still buzzing, but now she was pretty much consumed with thoughts of Jake Stein. No way, no way was she going to spend all that time in a car with him. One of them would surely end up in a body bag.

Cordelia also suspected that Jake had ulterior motives behind this favor. He was probably doing it just to see Molly again. Wait, maybe it's even more than that. Maybe he wants to get back together with her!

If that were true, then her whole family could be doomed. For some unknown reason, Molly had this big soft spot for Jake—she hadn't stayed friends with any of her exes, except for him. They had lost touch during college, but Molly and Jake had spent a lot of time together at school during senior year, to the point where everyone thought they were still going out. What if Jake professed his undying love for Molly and they got married and moved back into her parents' place together and ruined every single waking moment of Cordelia's life?

She inhaled the fresh scent of her shaving cream and tried to calm down. She was letting her imagination get the best of her. Molly was definitely over Jake. She was seeing a new guy every three weeks and living it up as usual. Actually, now that Cordelia thought about it, what had Molly seen in Jake in the first place? Molly used to claim that he was funnier than Dave Chappelle, but Cordelia had never seen any evidence of that. She just thought he was extremely obnoxious.

Jake Stein. She could see him now, but just barely. He was very nondescript and very blah looking. He was short for a guy—not more than five foot seven. He had shoulder-length hair and was a tad on the scrawny side. Not only did he have a crummy personality, he wasn't even that cute. Molly must have been going through some emotional or self-esteem crisis to consider dating him.

After her shower, Cordelia sat down at her desk and considered the situation with a clearer, cleaner body, mind, and soul. She knew her parents wouldn't force her to accept Jake's offer of a ride, but she figured they'd feel a lot better if she were traveling with someone they trusted, however misguided their presumptions about Jake might be. She knew her mother was already feeling guilty that she couldn't drive Cordelia up herself. Hmm.

Sitting on a Greyhound bus for twenty and a half hours with two transfers—how grubby would that make her feel? No chance to wash up or change into fresh clothes.

Using gas station restrooms, eating sandwiches that came out of machines. None of this was good at all. Wait a minute, Cordelia said to herself. Maybe I don't have to be on the road for that many hours straight with Jake.

She could break the trip up over several days. They could spend the nights in separate rooms at nice, respectable motels so that they could have downtime, which might prevent them from killing each other. If she turned up the tunes on her iPod, she wouldn't have to make much conversation with Jake in the car. This line of thought was making the situation seem a little more acceptable. She went to her desk and sat down in front of her PowerBook. She brought up the Google search she had downloaded from her Treo and clicked on the link for a map of the West Coast.

A wide smile crept across Cordelia's face. She knew that Yosemite National Park was somewhere between San Diego and Eureka, but she hadn't realized it was almost exactly the same distance from each of the two cities. It wasn't in a direct line—actually, it was way off to the east, closer to the Nevada border than the Pacific coast. But so what? She could see Paul! And if her parents were paying for the gas, Jake would just have to deal with going the way she wanted to go.